DARK GAMES

MICHAEL PERKINS

BLUE MOON BOOKS
NEW YORK

Published by
Blue Moon Books
841 Broadway, Fourth Floor
New York, NY 10003

ISBN 1-56201-160-X

Manufactured in the United States of America

1

On the prowl, he stood at the bar of the Subterranean Club, scanning the immense main room for signs of life. It was still early, but he was restless. The sharp edges of loneliness were cutting at him. Since going underground, he'd been on a long run across the country, and he was tired.

A bleary desperation kept his gaze trained on the tableaux of need and desire—of bondage and submission, whipping and fisting, exhibitionism and voyeurism—being enacted before him. He was fascinated, as always, by the subtleties in each presentation; but, as time froze, and no new players appeared, his impatience grew.

He studied each woman who entered the club, looking for signs of her in them—the rare one who knew what she wanted, and might be willing to pursue it to the limit. Her.

He was no longer certain that he would be able to recognize her if she appeared. Since they'd split, he'd sought her in countless theaters of the perverse. But night after night passed, and then month after month, and she didn't walk in.

Sometimes in his prowling he would encounter players who seemed to burn with the same crazy hot need that consumed him, but he was always disappointed by how little they were willing to risk. Most people didn't know what they wanted, and were too frightened to find out. They dabbled in the dark games and then drew back, fearful of being pulled in too deeply.

He ordered another vodka, and when he turned back around, saw a flurry of activity at the door, an influx of people, entrances being made. In their midst, but apart from them, stood a tall woman in a black cape, wearing a shiny rubber cat suit. Her height, augmented by her upswept hair and boots, was unusual; but it was her posture that drew his attention. It said she was in control—but her eyes said she was stepping down into the darkness.

She'd shown up at last. Not *her*, but one like her.

He wasn't a romantic. His certainty was more primitive. He was focused on her with such intense concentration that, like an animal, she sensed it and glanced his way. That willful, unguarded glare was the only opening he needed.

He closed his eyes, grateful that his waiting was over, relief replacing edginess as he allowed himself to imagine how her skin would smell, the weight of her breasts in his hands—even the smooth tautness of her thighs, as she opened herself for him.

2

Katherine Cooper stepped down into the darkness of the Subterranean Club on a Friday in January. It was close to midnight, and so cold outside her face ached from it. The warmth of the club was a welcoming embrace that drew her in.

She paused to let her eyes adjust to the dark spectacle before her and a crowd of celebrants pushed past, their excitement urging her deeper into the caliginous cavern. Her stiletto heel boots tapped softly on a concrete floor that was viscous and uneven, like a soft, undulant tongue. Fake smoke curled in tendrils around the hem of her long black cape. Flickering strobe lights made her blink. The pungent odors of sweat, semen and disinfectant widened her nostrils. Cacophonous electronic music piped in from another galaxy made her eardrums vibrate. She felt overwhelmed for just an instant—Alice down the rabbit hole. Even when she didn't know the rules of the game she had decided to play. Katherine was possessed with a self-confidence that could shatter glass. Besides, there was a first time for everything—even playing dominatrix. It was just another dress up game, she thought. A role.

3

With her head thrown back, she strode into the cave of illusion, where tall jagged mirrors placed at odd angles on the rough walls reflected startling images of men and women deeply involved in sexual rituals. In every scene there were onlookers wearing leather and vinyl, some of them dressed as policemen and military officers, and their expressions were severely expectant.

None of them missed her slow progress through the giant room. They were used to entrances, but she moved with a muscular, feline assurance that caused even the most blasé to step aside. Her auburn hair was piled artfully above a wide, chiseled face that, with its expressive large eyes and carved, lush mouth, was exotic—as if she came from another century. Under her sweeping, regal cape she wore a shiny tight black rubber suit, so that light caught in the curves of her tall, slender figure.

She ignored their admiring, curious stares, but when a group, gathered around a scene in progress, opened its ranks for her, she stopped to watch. A very large coffee colored man with a shaved head and pointed goatee, dressed in a Nazi uniform, was forcing a slightly bearded man dressed only in a leather vest and chaps to suck the butt end of a ferocious-looking riding crop. The Nazi cursed his slave in guttural German while some of the onlookers palmed their crotches. The submissive's buttocks were striped red.

Seeing that he'd lost the attention of the onlookers, the Nazi stepped back. The submissive's eyes widened when he looked up and saw Katherine. He shuffled to her on his knees to present himself for judgment. He dipped his head to lick the toes of her tall black boots, dulling their shine. Katherine hesitated only a moment before grinding the point of her heel into the soft meat of the back of his hand. He expelled his breath in a soft whinny of pleasure as she increased the pressure. The

4

gratitude in his moist eyes begged for more. Instead, she lifted her foot and allowed him to kiss the punishing heel. This time his worship was more restrained.

She looked around her, her impassive gaze betraying nothing of her inner feelings.

3

It was enough. She was satisfied. It was for this introduction that she had come. But when she turned to go, she was met with imploring looks from some of the men who had watched her. Two of the disappointed ones, more persistent, followed her when she headed for the bar. They plucked at her cape with their needs and hopes.

Then a large man in black leather—no supplicant for her freshness, or her strict attention, but rather a minatory lord—blocked their way. Seeing something in the man's face that was seriously disconcerting, her pursuers faded back into the shadows.

When he turned his strange eyes on her, Katherine struggled to maintain her composure. He was a tall, lean man, sharp as an ax blade, with wide shoulders and a prominent nose. He looked wolfish and hungry when he smiled.

"Why did you do that?" she asked, in her best haughty-bad-girl voice.

"The first rule of the game is, don't waste your time with people who don't matter. At least, not your first time out."

He spoke with a slight twang she couldn't place. California by way of the Rockies, she guessed.

"And you—you're the judge of who matters?"

He nodded and smiled again, as if this was self-evident.

"In places like this, yes."

"Maybe they were friends of mine. Admirers." She was coquettish.

He shook his head. "Bozos. Posers."

"I saw you staring. I don't like people staring at me."

"Then you shouldn't dress like that. Or come to places you can't handle all the way."

He saw a flicker of recognition at the corner of her mouth. It made him want to see her teeth. He liked good teeth. He wanted them to be white and regular.

"You're sure of yourself, aren't you?"

He looked around, as if to indicate his territory.

"It's my game."

Her sudden smile was devastating in a way he didn't expect. Her teeth were neat and small and white. Their sparkle excited him. She was a fresh American beauty open to the darkness.

"All right," she said, as if she'd settled things in her mind. "I think I would like a drink."

He ordered a double vodka without asking her preference, and when he offered it to her he held it away so that she had to reach out for it. She drank half of it quickly, without taking her eyes from him. Greasy long black hair, beard stubble—outlaw.

"What's your name?" She finished the drink while watching him.

He shook his head. "It doesn't matter."

"Well, thanks for the drink then." She put her empty glass on the bar and turned as if to leave, wanting to be called back.

"What's wrong?"

"I guess I won't be seeing you."

"Why do you say that?"

"You've got disappearance written all over you."

He bent his long body over the bar, borrowed a pencil, and stabbed jaggedly at a bar napkin. He pressed it into her hand.

"You can leave a message here—when you're ready."

"What does that mean?"

"It's up to you to decide."

She pretended ignorance. "What?"

"How far you want to take it."

She almost blurted out "*all the way—that's how I'm made*, but she bit her tongue, and tasted blood.

He gave her a look of complicity, as if he could read her mind; then he touched the tip of his finger to the shiny black rubber tip of her left breast, and was gone.

4

Pale, winter morning sunlight streamed through the tall windows of Katherine's Upper West Side apartment. When it struck her eyelids, she pulled the sheet over her head, and then both pillows. In the silvery blue world of her dream she was close to orgasm, tremblingly poised at the ragged edge of a wave about to break with crashing force. A fully clothed man stood over her wearing the beaked, feathered mask of a raptor. His blunt dark penis protruded from his zipper, and he was stroking it to full erection with a meditative deliberateness that excited her. She couldn't take her eyes from it, and her mouth filled with saliva. She was on her knees, naked bottom in the air, shamelessly exposing herself to him and to a woman she didn't recognize. In a hoarsely urgent voice he was giving her explicit commands to masturbate.

She awoke too soon. Making little mewing, kittenish sounds of disappointment, she fought free of the tangled sheets, pushed back the down coverlet, and stretched her long arms tiredly. She pressed her hand between her thighs, smearing the wetness, but it was too late. Sitting up in her king sized bed, she propped her pillows against the hard spindles of its sticklike mission headboard. The bed was an island that dominated her minimalist studio apartment, placed so that she faced floor to ceiling book-cases filled with college classics, publishers' freebies and two long shelves of eclectically collected erotica. How-to sex manuals squeezed shoulder to shoulder with works by Reage, Califia, Trocchi, Miller and anonymous biker slut fiction.

Religious art and antique crucifixes hung on one wall opposite the two windows admitting the sunlight that had awakened her. It gleamed dully on a polished wooden floor and a few pieces of mission furniture.

The last wisps of the dream dissipated as she came awake, leaving her feeling frustrated and half crazy. The dream, her debut at the Subterranean Club—it added up to desperation, from which there was no relief. The weekend lay before her, unplanned and disappointingly empty, once again, of sexual opportunities.

She supposed she was attractive—people always said so—and at twenty-seven she was still young, but there was no one in her bed with her. She was becoming in-creasingly obsessed with sex.

Couldn't men smell her need? Or was it simply that she had no time? Like many young women struggling to thrive in millennial Manhattan, she was trapped on the hamster wheel of ambition. She worked too hard. She lived a fast, complicated, compartmentalized life that was centered on her publishing career. She was a success, but the price was that she spent most of her rare free weekends alone.

Driven by the urgent prodding of her bladder, she staggered sleepily into her bathroom. Luxurious in a generous, Victorian sense, its royal size and apurte-nances were the reason she paid an inordinate rent for a studio apartment she could stride across in a minute.

Mirrors on each wall reflected thick towels, a vase of cut flowers, tall Chinese vases filled with dried flowers, her framed butterfly collection, and her Victorian erotic prints. (Her favorite was a large Beardsley of a small man sporting an erection bigger than himself.) Persian carpets decorated a black tile floor. Her giant bathtub sat in the center of this inner chamber like a steamy throne.

She peed, started a bath, donned a silk kimono with a dragon design, put coffee on, popped an English muffin in the toaster, and picked up *The New York Times* outside her door. A few steps here, a few steps there, and she had breakfast and bath together.

She sprinkled aromatic salts into the hot water and shrugged out of her kimono, casting a critical eye upon her reflection in the mirrors. But her cursory morning-after inspection turned up nothing amiss. She thought she was not beautiful, although perhaps striking; but she liked her long legs and graceful long feet, the firm thrust of her breasts, her mussed auburn hair. Her ass, plump and heart-shaped, was a secret treasure waiting for the right hands to discover it.

The smoke in her hair and the ache in her calves brought her adventure of the night before to mind. He stood before her again, a challenge in his eyes she couldn't interpret. She had been almost fluttery with him.

Sinking gratefully into the hot bubbles of her bath, she tried to figure out his appeal. One thing she was sure of, it was primitive. Maybe it was his eyes. One was a window on something wild and dark, but the other looked beyond her. At what? What did he see in her that she couldn't see?

Then she recalled the pressure of his fingertip on her rubber clad nipple, and how much of himself he had transmitted in that simple touch. *God, he was hot!*

Was she reading too much into their brief exchange?

She didn't think so. She had recognized him immediately as the rare, real thing—a man for whom sex came first. She was a connoisseur of such men, and each time she met one she slept with him. Her instinct was never wrong.

The good ones are like jungle predators, she thought. They're loners, and they don't stick around for long.

On the other hand, there were the beings in ties and trousers with whom she worked and socialized who seemed to be sexless. The secret contempt she felt for them enabled her to compete successfully with them. She wouldn't hesitate to step on their tiny balls if they stood between her and the achievement of her goals. Ruefully, she conceded that such strongly defined tastes in men inevitably led to empty weekends—and the inadequate solace of masturbation.

She propped her feet on the rim of the bathtub and reached for the nozzle of the shower attachment. Directing a forceful stream of water between her legs, she let her mind slip back to her most recent encounter with the real thing.

His name was Redmon—a tall, bearded Viking pirate who loved fast cars and sailboats, a sculptor with a loft in TriBeCa who made his living smuggling soft drugs and good pre-Columbian artifacts. When she met him at an art opening in Chelsea, she recognized him immediately for what he was. "I want it," was all she had to say to him. In the taxi to his loft he put two fingers inside her before he kissed her. As soon as his door closed behind them, he picked her up and threw her on his bed, fucking her so hard she thought the bed would break—or she would. All the while he was kissing her and chuckling delightedly—as if they shared a secret but profound joke. His joy, the tip of his tongue and the tip of his sex, completed an electrical circuit in her. The memory triggered her climax.

True to his kind, Redmon hadn't stuck around for long. A few weeks later, he'd sailed off to the Caribbean, and, except for a postcard now and then, had vanished from her life.

Post-orgasm, Katherine sipped the last of her cold coffee, while looking through the soggy *Times* for something to do with her weekend. The chirpy articles on fashions and trends bored and irritated her—she didn't have the time to be trendy!—but if she looked closely enough she knew she'd find something of interest. Manhattan's wonders were inexhaustible.

Her eye fell on a description of a new exhibit at the American Museum of Natural History. A show of living tropical butterflies was drawing crowds. The butterflies were contained in an enclosed habitat that replicated their natural environments.

Through a lonely childhood, Katherine had enjoyed a passionate interest in the myriad forms life takes. She played with snakes and skunks, spiders and butterflies. She especially gravitated to animals that others avoided. She liked the mystery of not being able to know them. Not ever. She knew she was strange.

Over the years, she had come to realize that a deep perversity ruled the core of her being. She could be as ruthless in her evaluation of herself as she was of others—and from what she saw, people were as unknown as animals except for scattered brief moments during sex. They didn't have a clue as to whom they were. She did.

The butterfly article gave her an idea. She rinsed, and wrapped herself in a fluffy bath towel. There in the corner of the bathroom lay her rubber suit and crumpled black cape. Quickly, she found the napkin he'd written his phone number on. His handwriting was a series of stark Gothic slashes, a cruel calligraphy that beckoned to her because she sensed its challenge: *stay away unless you're serious.*

Maybe she was seriously crazy, but she decided she *was* serious.

She punched in the number and got an answering machine with a voice on it not his. "Star here. Leave your name and number, and maybe we'll get back to you."

She inhaled deeply. "Okay. This is for the man I met at the Subterranean Club last night. I'm going to the Museum of Natural History today. There's an exhibit of live butterflies, you know, like they fly around, and I like butterflies, so...."

The machine clicked off before she coulld finish. She hung up, wondering why she hadn't said she just wanted to see him again. She knew, it was about power. Relations between the sexes was a game of call and response, advance and retreat, boldness and coyness, seduction and withdrawal, dominance and submission. People were just furless animals playing power games. Most played the eternal mating game. Only a few of them, mavericks and outlaws, the passionate and the curious, played the dark games because they yearned to become more human.

5

Katherine sallied forth from her apartment in the early afternoon. It was a fair, cold day with little flurries of snow that dissipated before reaching the pavement. She headed across town to Columbus Avenue, which she knew would be crowded with shoppers and couples seeking a late lunch.

On the avenue she strolled Uptown to the museum, people-watching and window shopping, dressed for warmth in a yellow vinyl trench coat that had cost her a week's pay and comfortable in low pumps. Her hair glistened with snowflakes. She stopped to look in the window of a shop that sold animal bones as jewelry, and then in a bakery for a roll to eat while walking. At a cross street she paused to inspect the menu posted outside a new restaurant, Le Papillon, that she thought she might try for an early dinner. The special was one of her favorites, frog's legs in garlic butter.

She didn't think he would show up, but she felt more than the usual anticipatory thrill as she mounted the stone steps of the great museum. Since her childhood, Katherine had always walked through its doors with feelings of awe and expectation. As a child, she came to the museum to satisfy her boundless curiosity about the natural world. Later, she had discovered that it was also a wonderful place to cruise for a pickup—not as fruitful as one of the art museums perhaps, but more likely to attract the kind of lovers she looked for. She had picked up a few memorable one night stands in its brightly polished marble halls. In many ways, it was her natural habitat, she thought.

She wandered aimlessly in the museum, reluctant to go straight to the butterflies. She sat on the bench beneath a herd of charging elephants forever stopped in their tracks, surrounded on all sides by dioramas of frozen animal life, each scene engraved in her memory— part of her fantasy life.

The wolves in the Arctic tundra, for instance, was one of the scenes. She glanced over at it and saw a troop of cub scouts milling around the diorama. Six months before, she had been gazing into it, placing herself in the tableau, first the hunted, then the hunter. Garson had come up behind her and began talking to her reflection in the glass. Trying to whisper, he growled. He was large and bulky, like a grizzly bear with his thick spiky hair and silver beard.

"They've got it all wrong, you know. All these years, and they haven't changed it." He shook his head in mock disgust, but there was mischief in his eyes.

"What did they get wrong?" she asked.

"The sky is not like that—not at that time of year." She turned to face him. "How do you know?"

"I was stationed there, when I was in the Navy."

He said he'd come to check something out about New Guinea, where he was traveling to collect botanical specimens. She liked his enthusiasm, his grand gestures when he spoke of exploration, his large hands. An hour later, they were on her big bed. His caresses began gently

enough, but when they turned harder, she found to her surprise that she liked to be spanked.

This was a politically inconvenient discovery that changed the course of her life, and began the process of development that led to her appearance at the Subterranean Club.

And to him. What if he did show up, she mused, and he was different? He belonged in that dark cavern. Would he be so sure of himself on the street in daylight, or in a museum?

Refusing to rush to disappointment, she walked slowly through the museum to the Hall of Oceanic Birds, where the butterfly vivarium had been installed.

She waited patiently in a long line, and, once inside the exhibit, immediately shed her trench coat. The moist heat rose like steam from a heavy wool blanket. She was transfixed by the fantastic, flickering life above her head. Four hundred butterflies fluttered in the curtain of tropical greenery the museum had constructed. She didn't see him.

One of her first entomological passions had been lepidopteran, and especially the fabulous blue *Morphos* butterflies she studied on Cape Cod. She knew that the colorful wings of most butterflies served as a danger signal to predators: *I'm poisonous, don't eat me*. She also knew that the brilliant hues of the male blue morphos sent a sex signal. Wings folded, morphos were disguised in drab; but when they took flight, she could no more take her eyes off them than she could avert her gaze from an exposed penis.

While she stood there lost in thought, a morpho did a little dance before her eyes, and then—just as she reached up to scratch her nose—landed on her wrist. She held her arm still, in midair, hypnotized by this tiny bit of grace.

Then, just as suddenly as it had landed, the blue butterfly launched itself on an updraft of air. Before she could lower her arm, a strong hand clamped her wrist like a handcuff.

Startled from her trance, Katherine turned.

It was him, smiling tightly, as if more would put a crack in his angular face. His grip loosened, but he drew her toward him and she did not resist. He wore a black leather coat that made him look armored and out of place. He seemed relaxed, however, if bemused, by his surroundings, but she couldn't read him. She looked into his eyes for reassuring warmth and saw ice burning.

"I didn't know if you would come. I must have looked stupid last night."

"You looked new, not stupid."

"What if you didn't like butterflies?"

"If I say call when you're ready, then I'll come. Count on it. I've been looking for you for a long time. From way before last night."

"Nothing happens by accident, then."

"No."

He released her wrist, but she didn't step away from him. That moment for her was like peering down a dark tunnel through which a hot wind howled—drowning out even the tape-recorded noises of screeching monkeys and parakeets in the background. There was only the tunnel, at the end of which loomed a convergence she could not make out. There was only the future, into which she was being drawn by an inexorable force.

She breathed deeply several times and told herself that she was still in control—that she could still choose to walk away.

She glanced at him. He was scary. More than she bargained for.

Walk away. Just walk away.

But she imagined his hands on her body. They would open her like a book. They would read her needs as if reading Braille. Just standing next to his solidity she could imagine him deep inside her and feel his pubic bone rubbing against hers.

Just think of him as a date, she told herself. She closed her eyes, feeling faint, and touched his sleeve.

"I'm hungry. Do you want to go get something?" she asked weakly. He nodded: whatever.

Maybe if she had more time to be with him, she'd know what to do. Maybe if she ate, she'd then be strong enough to decide.

6

At Le Papillon they descended a winding iron staircase into a large, white-tiled room with a zinc bar. Groups of laughing people sat at long wooden tables. The bustle and good cheer pleased neither of them, and they turned to go. A harried young *maitre d'* called them back, and led them across the room and up a flight of wooden stairs. They were ushered into a narrow, quiet room lined with wooden booths. He lit a candle on their table, took her order for wine, and left them alone. Katherine took a seat facing the door and was surprised when her date slid in next to her.

"I'm glad we're not out there," she said into the silence that had fallen between them since leaving the museum. She didn't look at his profile, but at his hands resting on the table. They were large and square tipped, and the nails were trimmed very short. She liked big men with big hands. She stole a glance at him. He looked like a hick, she thought, from way out of town. But he was also, somehow, almost sinister. A gangster hick. Punk cowboy. Outlaw. She guessed he felt out of place, but he didn't look uncomfortable. It was as if he was aware of everything that happened around him, while remaining oblivious of its normal meaning.

While she looked at her menu he watched her with the patient, expectant expression of a jungle animal in a diorama at the museum observing its prey. It was unnerving, but exciting.

When their wine came, she ordered the house special, *Grenouilles a la Laconnaise*, and he asked what it was.

"It's frog's legs made with garlic butter," the waiter told him, while opening the wine and flirting a little.

"I'll pass."

Being in a restaurant ordering food made her feel more in control. She lifted her glass and sipped. The wine warmed her. She was emboldened to make a declaration to him.

"I want you to know something. If anything happens— I mean, between us—it will be because I want it to."

"It wouldn't be right, otherwise," he agreed, sure of himself.

"I can't figure you out."

"It's more fun if you don't even try."

"You're different, but I don't know if that's good or bad."

"I'll show you how good." He was not being glib—it was a promise he was making to her.

"I don't know anything about you."

"Well," he drawled, looking around him. "I'm not at my best in a French restaurant or in museums."

"Where are you at your best?"

"Any place we're alone together."

She took another sip of her wine, at a loss for something further to say that would set boundaries between them—that would allow her to remain in control of the situation.

While feeling those hands on her body.

"You don't know what to do, do you?" he asked her. She nodded helplessly.

"You know, butterflies only live two or three weeks. I guess that's why they're always moving around. They can't afford to waste any time. They take chances."

"What do you know about butterflies?"

"I can read a sign like anybody else. Even a book, once in awhile."

"So, 'live fast, die young'—is that your motto?"

"I don't know about dying. But I like it that they don't waste time."

Her dish arrived. The waiter presented her frog's legs with a flourish, replenished their wine glasses, and left them alone again. She was famished, and the little white legs looked succulent.

She reached for her fork, but once again his fingers closed over her wrist.

"Let me," he said. It wasn't quite a command, yet it was stronger than an invitation. She stubbornly shook her head, instinctively rebelling.

"I'm not a child. Don't ever treat me like one."

"Open," he commanded, ignoring her. She relented.

He fed her slowly and deliberately, totally focused on her, using the edge of her napkin to keep the butter from smearing her chin, watching her even white teeth tear the tiny morsels of juicy flesh.

"I'm not a. . . ." she started to say again when he had fed her.

"No, you're not a child, and I'm not your daddy. But when I'm with you, I own you. You're mine. That means that everything you do, you'll do because I want it that way."

7

Hand on his arm, she had to take little half steps to keep up with him. He waited until they were inside the lobby of her building before he kissed her. His lips were hard and cold, but he made his mouth soft and wet and then hers and the kiss went on and on. The tip of his tongue moved over her teeth. Too late, she thought of the garlic on her breath. Her vinyl coat made its creaky vinyl sound against his leather coat.

She told him her apartment was a walkup. He grinned, almost.

"Let me take your coat, then." Puzzled, she shrugged out of it, feeling dizzy—not from the wine, but from the long kiss.

"I want to watch you climb the stairs," he explained, adding, "Take off your underpants, too."

Too surprised to question him, she took his arm as she removed the garment. He stuffed it into his pocket.

She started up the stairs. Not having given any thought to the act of stair climbing since she was five, she felt awkward, conscious of his focus on the movement of her ass under her tight skirt. But if it was wiggle he wanted, she gave him a good show, slowing at each small landing to exaggerate the roll of her hips, feeling at first liberatingly slutty, and then embarassed.

In the apartment he waited as she lit candles and pulled curtains closed, his skeptical gaze taking in the large bed, the rows of books, and the religious art on her walls, frowning at the latter.

"What's the matter?" she asked, seeing his face darken.

"Nothing," he replied, but his glare made it plain that he disapproved.

"I'm not religious, if that's what you're thinking. I collect them as art pieces." She kept to herself what else they meant to her.

"Art." He paused, wonderingly, to consider this possibility. "I guess you might call them that. You can call things any name you want, can't you?"

His intensity once again made her nervous. She went into the bathroom without bothering to close the door—whatever was about to happen, it was too late to back out now, she thought. She stood before a mirror fussing with her hair, and he came up behind her. Their eyes locked in the mirror, a silver lake that drew them into its depths.

"I warn you, my only problem is my dirty mind," she said, in an attempt at bravado.

He didn't blink, but leered almost frighteningly.

"I hope so. I sincerely hope so."

She whirled, as if to take him by surprise, smiling in ironic mock submission as she whispered, "Don't you want to fuck me?"

He surprised her by shaking his head. "Not yet. I want to see your ass first. Get down on the floor and take off your skirt."

She saw that she had no choice but to obey. She'd

24

accepted his terms in the restaurant, and the games were starting, she'd play.

She sank to her knees.

"Just skinny out of your skirt. I want to see that beautiful butt high up in the air. Yes, that's pretty enough to give a dead man a hard-on. Now play with yourself. I want to see that, too."

"Don't you want to go to bed? I'll show you everything there."

"I want to see that," he repeated firmly.

So, kneeling on a rug, cheek pressed against cool tile, left hand supporting this awkward position, Katherine reached between her legs and pushed three fingers into her vagina. She breathed in little panting gasps that she hoped he wouldn't hear. The engorged shaft of her clitoris readily responded to her touch, but what excited her was knowing that he was watching her as she got off.

That—and her own shamelessness, perhaps.

"Aren't you going to fuck me? Come on, I want you to fuck me," she whispered hoarsely, making a final effort to sound seductive and still in control. But her plea fell on deaf ears. He shook his head.

"You're not ready yet. You need some of this."

Without warning, he struck her upturned ass, and she collapsed onto her rug, feeling a powerful surge of heat in her sex. She quickly rose to face him with a sense of welcome dread, here he was at last, not Death but Life, quickening.

The blow had been too hard. Too presumptuous, too soon, too—

But it had pushed her up to, the next level, to where she'd never climbed except in dreams.

"You've got to fuck me."

"You don't want it badly enough yet."

"What do I have to do?" She didn't hold back the frustrated disappointment in her voice.

He shook his head. "Unh unh. You're used to having things your own way. That's got to change."

She looked down at herself. There she was, breasts heaving, nipples stiff, exposed from the waist down, still tingling from the near orgasmic impact of his hand. *Her own way*?

How did he know this was the game she wanted to play?

"Let me at least see your penis then."

"You're not ready for it."

But instead of teasing her further, he unzipped, and introduced himself to her all over again.

She sucked in air, defensively, stricken with stunned disbelief. Finally, she blurted out the obvious: "That is a fucking dragon." Gaping at it.

Her new lover was so generously endowed he was in his own, priapic, class. His uncircumsized penis, long, thick and purplish, was so big that she wondered for a moment if it wasn't a dildo he had stuffed in his pants as a joke. Something to scare the girls with.

"No wonder . . . you're so sure of yourself."

Her reaction seemed to please him. He laughed for the first time. "Meet the boss. I just do what he wants."

As if the surprising organ was not attached to him, as if the rest of him was merely a support system for it. She had known a few men who behaved that way, and reveled in their unabashed randiness; but never one so justified in his pride of ownership.

Somehow this surprise put her need in perspective. While her rational mind acknowledged the comic absurdity of sex—its often grotesque positions, shameless lust, surreal disregard for balance and control, the manipulation and submission, the mess—and shuddered, she saw in looking at his penis how desire destroys the proportions of things. How imperative its demands were.

"Get down on the floor again," he ordered.

She obeyed with a sigh, yearning to touch the semi-erection he idly fondled. But it was his scenario they would play out. It would be her turn later. . . .

Once again he spanked her, this time more lightly, and expertly introduced a fingertip into the tight center of the rose between her ass cheeks. She winced, but it felt good. She hoped he wasn't going to try to put his penis in there—not even the tip.

"Close your eyes." She did so reluctantly, and he immediately fixed a blindfold over them. She protested feebly, and he put a silencing finger to her lips.

"I want to see. . . ." she gasped. Once again the absurdity of it struck her. She was kneeling in her bathroom, butt in the air, blindfolded, being spanked by a strange man who might harm her—and she was doing so willingly!

She listened to slight noises as he moved around the bathroom. She heard him splash his urine loudly in the toilet, wash his hands—and then some vigorous movement as if he was playing with himself as he stood over her.

"Ow!" she exclaimed. He was using her hairbrush, bristles down, to scratch her buttocks, and then he turned it over to spank her with it. She felt a wonderful warmth licking at her vulva and rising in her belly. His tempo increased, the blows became harder, but she was beyond pain, in any ordinary sense.

Then he did a surprising thing. Kneeling, he lifted her into his arms, cradling her burning buttocks against the cold leather of his vest, and carried her out of the bathroom to her bed. He was very strong, and his breathing was even and regular.

She stiffened when he put her down onto the softness of the bed. "Relax," he told her.

"The blindfold."

"No—leave it on a little while longer."

His hands lifted and parted her thighs, and she felt his mouth on her, his hard lips that softened so quickly, the bristles of his beard. He pushed his long tongue into her tight pink opening—thrusting deep inside and then withdrawing to lick and suck her clitoris.

"Play with your titties," he ordered, and she pushed her hands under her sweater to massage her breasts, squeezing her stiff nipples so that soon the feelings in the tips of her breasts matched the oscillating excitement in her groin. Somehow he slowed down and drew out each movement of his lips and tongue so that time was suspended between the waves of her orgasm. Her thighs trembled and her back arched as she came.

She heard herself shouting obscenities she never spoke aloud as if someone else was shouting them. Her hands beat on his bony shoulders. Her inner thighs were wet.

He left the bed after she had stopped moving. When he returned, he removed the blindfold and offered her a washcloth he'd soaked in hot water. When she didn't take it from him, he proceeded to dab gently at the soreness between her legs.

He sat facing her on the bed, beaming with a kind of boyish, Mephistophelean delight at the pleasure he'd given her. His left hand grasped his penis like a rudder. His ship was her big bed, and he was captain.

"I don't even know what to call you," she said at last. "It's not supposed to be this good, this fast, with someone you don't know."

"Call me anything you want to. It's not important."

"Don't you have a name?"

"I'm invisible. Invisible people have no names."

"You're crazy, too," she laughed. Thinking how vividly he stood out.

"Something like that, you could say."

"You are the strangest man I've ever gone to bed with."

"I've heard that before."

"Jesus Christ," she exclaimed. "You've had your finger up my ass, and I don't know anything about you."

"One thing I can tell you," he said dryly. "My name ain't Jesus Christ."

With this, he gazed up at the crucifixes on her walls, his tightly downturned mouth expressing a mixture of disdain and fear that was chilling.

"What have you got against crosses?"

"It's what they stand for."

"Don't you believe in God?" It wasn't the conversation she expected to be having after being made love to.

"I believe in what we just did. Sex is what I believe in. It's what I do, what I'm good at, and what I think about most."

"It's just a symbol. A cross is just a symbol."

"You like those two sticks for a symbol? Excuse me, but I prefer the old pole and hole," he said with intense feeling. He made the universal sign of sex for her, finger moving into circled fingers. "I prefer my tongue in your pussy."

"It's like you've got a personal grudge," she said, shaking her head. "I don't understand."

"It is personal. Take my word for it."

"You're scaring me."

"No I'm not. You just don't know what to call it."

"Let's not talk anymore. I just want you to fuck me with that monster dick."

"You like it?"

She moved closer to touch it, taking it in both hands and stroking its silky arrogance. Reaching between his thighs, she hefted his testicles.

"May I kiss it?" She was girlish.

"Yes. Kiss it. Let me feel those cocksucker's lips fit around the head."

She moistened her lips and sprawled prone on her bed, her hands on his knees. She had good reason to pride herself on her skills—no one had ever complained—but she'd never been presented with such a challenge. She delicately touched the tip of her tongue to the meaty glans of his penis and hesitated when she tasted salty pre-come. She thought guiltily about condoms and realized that it was already too late to think about protection, and that she had committed herself and entered the tunnel.

Besides, no latex would fit over his dragon.

It was irresponsible, it was stupid, it was dangerous, but she couldn't stop now. She stretched her lips over the mushroom cap of his penis, holding his thick shaft in both hands as her tongue penetrated his urethra. He stroked her hair, encouraging her to take more of him into her mouth, but she couldn't do it without choking.

"I know you'll be able to take it," he whispered obscenely, "I can tell from your mouth that you've given a lot of head."

She took no offense at his crudeness, because he was so comfortable with his sexuality that she felt strangely empowered. His freedom turned her on.

"It's too big. I can't. Come and fuck me, please. I think I can take it all the way in my pussy."

"I don't know if you're ready for it."

"Oh, please—just put it in me. Don't talk all day. Just fuck me."

It was what she had been waiting for, his hard body against her softness, his weight welcome. He lifted her calves to his shoulders so that she was open to receive him, and pushed slowly into her, stopping to let her adjust to the fullness, then pushing deeper until she was filled. He gasped at her tightness.

He began to move then, his weight on his elbows, big hands covering her breasts, fingers pinching her nipples. She pulled him into her, hands at his buttocks and his neck as they kissed. He feasted on her breasts, kissing and sucking and squeezing them, kissed her shoulders, and pushed up her arms so he could kiss and lick her armpits. He slowly withdrew the entire length of his penis and then plunged it deep inside her. Once he pulled all the way out, and she gasped in disappointment; until she felt him banging his glans against her clitoris, smacking it so that she could hear the wet sound and the pressure inside her began to build precipitously.

"Oh, you're fucking me so sweet, don't stop. . . ."

"You want it, don't you? You want it all."

"I want it all."

"You're my slut, aren't you?"

"Yes, I'm your slut. Just don't stop doing me."

"And you'll suck me off when I want you to? You'll learn how to do it right?"

"You can have my mouth, you can have my pussy, you can have my ass. I just don't think I can take it all the way in my mouth."

"I'll show you," he promised. "Don't worry, I'll show you."

This exchange, breathed into each other's ears, excited them further, and he resumed his pounding into her.

"Move your ass," he ordered, and she swiveled her ass, arching her pelvis to meet his thrusts, reflecting his energy back at him, so absorbed in the pleasure that suffused every aching cell that she could not form syllables. Impossibly, she felt him grow bigger inside her and the sensation sent her over the edge. Then he thrust deeply, stiffened his body, and howled as she felt hot semen spurt against her cervix.

Katherine had never had a more intense sexual experience; she felt savagely good, like a sated animal, as they lay beside each other breathing in ragged gasps, limp and yet deeply energized. Her apprehension about his strangeness was replaced now by a determination to hold onto him. Somehow, she would master him by a submission that would yet keep something back—some essential part of her strong, contrary nature. By being clever, she could keep him.

"Man, oh man," he crowed. "We could be underground with the woodchucks, and instead we're doing this."

"That's a morbid thought." Where was he coming from?

"Maybe so, but it's just a fact. I think about dying every time I come. It makes me feel like I'm winning."

"You're weird. Why would you think of death after you come? That's pretty extreme."

"I am extreme. Everything that happens tells me I should be."

"What do you mean?"

"You don't want to know." But she could tell that if she pressed, he would talk about himself. She didn't know if she wanted to hear it. From all the signs, she was likely to learn something about him that would be deeply perverse. Something frightening.

Then it came to her. If she was going to keep this man, ignorance was bliss. The less she knew about him, the better. Let him remain a mask to her, someone she would know solely from her own direct experience of him. As long as she didn't know his history, she could play any game he wanted and still remain in control. He would belong to her because he would be her creation. She wouldn't fear her own creation.

"I don't want to know anything about you," she told him. "I just want you to come back to me."

8

After sleeping twelve hours straight with Katherine in his arms, he felt renewed. He was back in the games, and things looked fresh again.

The cocaine made him talkative.

"I think she's open to just about anything—she's got a real spirit. There's a look in her eyes that keeps flashing a *yes* sign. You know what I mean?"

Eyebrows lifted, Star listened, patiently cynical, the way he always was. When he wrinkled his brow—which he did often—it was to mock some new folly. The effect was to push together the five-pointed star tattooed between his shaggy eyebrows so that it looked like a third eye glaring at you.

They sat across from each other in Star's new loft on East Houston Street, knocking back Dos Equis and loosening up. On a wide coffee table between them sat empty bottles and a silver tray laden with choice pharmaceuticals.

Thoroughly soundproofed, the loft was kept permanently dark with heavy curtains. Clients flew in from Liverpool and Munich, Chicago and Nashville, to have Star ink them with one of his Asterion Studio originals, and he liked to keep his business private. Wherever he moved, they followed, making his studio a nexus of the tribal underground. When his old friend Buddy Tate showed up looking beat, Star gave him shelter.

"Maybe sometimes you should pass," Star rumbled when Buddy paused. "Check to see if I've got this straight: in this deal, you get a player you can train who's more than willing, and she gets to live out some mystery man fantasy, the kind chicks have. She may let you walk her on a leash, if you want, but you're just some anonymous stud to her. . . . Is that about it?"

He looked questioningly at Buddy, and didn't wait for his response. "Sounds like a match made in hell. Just like with Robin."

"Difference is, she's not Robin. She's not crazy like Robin."

Star handed him another Dos Equis. "Well, we'll see. We'll see, Buddy. A woman like this is powerful juju."

"Anyway, I don't want to get too close to her. I just want to stretch it out and see how far it goes."

"Maybe this one—what's her name? Katherine?— just doesn't know her true nature yet. You have to watch out for spider women—they're everywhere."

It was Star's theory, often repeated, that the most seductive women players were like those female spiders who eat their male sex partners after mating. That the price of sex with them was death.

"Katherine's not one of them, I'm telling you. She's too naive. Do you know what she said to me? That she had a dirty mind—she said it just like she knew what that meant."

"Before I know it, you'll be using that four letter word again. If I hear it coming from you, I'll have to wash your mouth out."

"What do you mean?"

Star made a flicking motion with his long fingers, as if warding off some winged evil: "The word is *love*, Buddy."

"Yeah, I know. Spell it backwards. . . . Fuck you, man."

Star laughed and reached into the cushions behind him for his .22 target pistol. He kept it there ready for spontaneous target shooting, self-defense, emphasis at the end of an argument, or to summon service. Buddy stuck his fingers in his ears, shaking his head at his friend's eccentricity. He knew about guns, had used them in a past life, and now wanted nothing to do with them.

"We need more beer," Star explained, firing a round into the ceiling, which was already riddled with holes.

"I don't know whether you're a genius, or fucking crazy."

"It works—watch."

His signal was answered by the appearance of a young woman in a black *bustier* and hot pants. She had cropped red hair, piercings in her left nostril, lips and tongue, and she wore an iron collar around her neck. Her name was Cyd, and she had shown up at the loft one evening shortly after Star arrived in New York, offering to be his house slave in return for tattoo work.

The first time Buddy saw her, he thought she was ugly, partly because her eyes were slightly crossed and her nose had been broken; but mostly because half of her perfect body was covered with a purple birthmark, and the other half was quickly being filled in with tattoos. It was a fierce look, truly tribal. But after awhile, he saw that she was beautiful, after all. She could be studied like a living painting.

She was also the best submissive Star had ever found. She enjoyed her service so much she wore her iron collar on the streets of the Lower East Side like a badge of honor.

"We need more beer, sugar," Star told her, returning his pistol to the cushions behind him.

She nodded. "More blow?" she inquired politely, glancing at the coffee table. Her mouth made a perfect O, which caused a twinge in Buddy's groin. Star's mind was running along the same track.

"Nah. I want to be able to get it up."

Cyd smiled, cutely wicked, and ran the tip of her tongue over her lips, as if polishing her black lipstick. She nodded again, and went for the beer. When she returned, she set the brown bottles before them on the coffee table, and waited for Star's next direction. All he had to do was point to the table.

She climbed onto it and raised her arms gracefully, turning slowly around so that both men could savor her tautly perfect, illustrated body. First she removed her bustier. Her small breasts jutted forth, capped by puffy pink nipples that were soon hard. She cupped and squeezed the firm flesh for them.

Buddy's hand fell to his crotch. Cyd's strip act on the coffee table never failed to make his bone stone. Star unzipped his pants.

Cyd pushed her hot pants down over her plump thighs, over her round bubble butt, down over the black stockings and garter belt that were never-to-be-removed parts of her uniform. She bent over to give them a long, slow look at her ass, still striped from a caning Star had given her the day before.

Stoned, they admired her artistry and the way her birthmark covered one of the cheeks of her ass, while the other was heraldic with astrological symbols designed by Star as she lay on his tattoo table. But what fascinated Buddy was a new tattoo—one still waiting to be filled in—of a large blue butterfly on her lower back. It was so recent he could see drops of dried blood.

"I like that butterfly," Buddy said, thinking, *once you see something one time, you see it everywhere. It's a sign.*

"Yeah, I know," Star said. "You told me about it."

Cyd arched her body backwards so that her palms touched the table and her legs were spread wide—displaying her shaved vulva, moist and red like a succulent fruit.

Buddy unzipped. He remembered what came next in Cyd's dance. She was able to squeeze her vaginal muscles so tightly that her tiny glabrous opening contracted as if around a penis.

"That's hot," Buddy said. New York had its sights, but Cyd's act was the best he'd seen so far. The winking orifice was wet.

"Never fails, does it?"

Star clapped his hands and Cyd got down from the table, kneeling between Star's legs. Buddy stroked himself, watching.

She spat into her hand and grasped her master's penis, expertly stroking him, stopping, spitting again so he was well lubricated, stroking him until he was fully erect. This attention was preliminary to the most amazing cock worship Buddy had seen since his arrival on the East Coast.

First she made obeisance to Star's big balls, which were absolutely hairless as a result of the shaving ceremonies they performed each week. She took each stone in her mouth, flicking it with the piercing on her tongue, while a forefinger played with his anus. She stretched his prick with her hand, long black fingernails scraping gently at his urethra. After she'd mouthed and nibbled at his balls, she began to lick straight up and down his shaft, concentrating on the prominent vein that throbbed there. Her movements were slow and methodical, her eyes on Star's response. When she took his glans in her mouth, he emitted a grunt of satisfaction. As she slowly swallowed his erection, he began a low humming noise, and stroked her cropped red hair. Although Buddy had witnessed this ritual twice before, it still excited him to impatient envy. He masturbated while waiting his turn.

The level of Star's humming increased dramatically as Cyd moved her head faster, and with a ululation of relief and ecstasy he came. Cyd's cheeks puffed out with the amount of it—too much to swallow—and semen dripped over her chin when Star pulled out.

She rested, still kneeling, her eyes going to Buddy's larger organ as if hypnotized by his hand as it moved up and down.

"Looks like you could use some help with that, Buddy," Star said, in invitation, winking and taking a sip of his beer.

Cyd repeated her performance with Buddy—with one necessary adjustment. When it came time to take him into her throat, she indicated that he should stand at the end of the couch while she lay back on it, neck arched like a swan, mouth open to swallow him whole. She had explained that it was a trick she'd learned from an old porno film.

Hands covering her hard little breasts, Buddy bent his long torso so that his dragon slid in and out of Cyd's black lipsticked mouth and down her lubricated throat without encountering a gag reflex. His balls bumped softly against her cheeks.

She was truly amazing. He closed his eyes and abandoned himself to the delicious sensations she was able to cause with her tongue and throat muscles. As he slid in and out of her mouth, he thought of Katherine's reluctance to give him such delight.

Well, she could learn. He would have to be patient but strict.

He felt the electricity building in his spine, felt it gather to surge through his penis and at last discharge, and he growled as it did—shooting his ecstasy straight down her throat. Afterwards he stood shuddering, letting her clean him off with her tongue, feeling her piercing scraping his shaft. When she finished, she went to crouch at Star's feet. Her face was inscrutable, but she licked her black lips with obvious pride in her work.

She's on another wavelength, Buddy thought. She made up her own rules, pursued her own goals, and remained unknowable except through sex. It was the way the hot ones were.

All that he knew of women came from having sex with them, and in all his experience he'd found no reason to believe that they were any different from men in their sexual cores. Believing this, he saw that it was his mission to help them to get down to their hot spots, which he envisioned as being like the molten core at the center of the earth. It was miles and miles down, and the only evidence of it on the surface were volcanoes erupting and earthquakes, but it was there. No matter how peaceful things seemed, the molten core was roaring like a blast furnace.

He looked at Cyd. She was sitting between his legs with her head on his thigh, as he stroked her hair. Her inscrutable, slightly crossed eyes were glazed over in reverie, lost in a space where they could not follow.

"Scary, isn't it?" Star asked, reading Buddy's thoughts. "She does what I tell her, but no one gets to her. She's walking down her own street. But it's not in our neighborhood—it's on another planet."

Buddy shook his head. "She's just like us. She just comes at what she wants from a different angle. She got off."

Cyd looked at him and smiled, licking her lips.

9

Katherine found it difficult to step back into Monday's workday world. Entering the gleaming Times Square skyscraper that housed her publishing company, Global Content, Inc., crowding into the elevator, mechanically greeting co-workers clutching briefcases and takeout coffee, was like entering a dreamworld. After the weekend, with its confirmation of the existence of a sexual dimension she had previously only fantasized, it was desire that was real, not work.

Her small office—she had recently been promoted out of cubicle hell—was cluttered with projects calling for her attention. A table was piled with promotional material in various stages of preparation. It was her job to shepherd the important ones into the media spotlight, and she enjoyed it. She found it exciting.

Now she contemplated the piles of papers and photos blankly. They were irrelevant to the inner world that was opening.

She had to force herself to get busy, spending the morning answering her E-mail, phoning bookers and buyers and editors, and planning her schedule for the week. In her encounters with her co-workers, she shared the elliptic gallows humor that was necessary for survival in corporate life, but she didn't mention the weekend. How could she describe it so they would understand?

She was contemplating this when Christian called her in for a meeting. With his long, sleek head, pencil line mustache, and nocturnal habits, she thought of her boss as a weasel.

There was pain in his beady black eyes. He lifted a heavy manuscript and dropped it. Picked it up and dropped it again.

"Good morning," she said briskly and cruelly.

"Do you have an aspirin?"

"Suffering again, Chris? Too much party-party?"

"I'm fucking serious, Katherine."

She had come prepared. She handed him three of the white tabs, and he popped them with his coffee.

"You are one mean bitch, Katherine."

"That's precisely why I've got your job sewn up."

He smiled painfully, head in his hands. It was true that he was being transferred to a more prestigious position in the London offices of GCI, but her cockiness about her prospects was not fitting. Where the hell was she coming from?

"Did you get laid or something?" he said with jealousy in his voice.

"Or something." She wouldn't give him the satisfaction of revealing anything about her private life. She could imagine how Christian would sneer if he saw her with her stranger.

"Well, I'm still here, and I've got a hoop for you to jump through."

"Just tell me how high I should jump," she said resignedly. His fatuous smirk told her he was dumping something big in her lap. "Act like a boss, boss."

"You know we've signed Olivier de Carlo?"

"It's on the grapevine—not to mention the *Times* and *Publishers Weekly*." De Carlo was a French aristocrat whose huge financial success with hedge funds was eclipsed by his celebrity status as a race car driver and playboy suitor of Hollywood actresses. There were nasty rumors about him that he was recklessly, scandalously, willing to elaborate upon in his memoirs. They were sufficiently explicit to initiate a bidding war, won preemptively by GCI, as usual.

"Well, he's in town, and he wants to consult about the publicity campaign for his book."

"Yes?"

"I'm off to London, which makes him your headache, sweetheart."

Instead of shouting at him, Katherine let out a protracted sigh. "Another last minute rush?"

Christian smiled. "Aren't they all? But if you want this office, you'll handle it with your usual super efficiency."

He held the heavy manuscript out to her.

"He's staying at the Gibbons-Wakely. I'd suggest you call him and set up a meeting."

Back in her office, she cleared her desk and sat down with a sandwich and the manuscript, which was entitled *My Life as a Monster*. Two hours later she looked up from it, shaking her head. The writer had succeeded in returning her to the sexual dimension of the weekend. Olivier de Carlo had led a vividly interesting life, both in public and in private, and he recounted his sexual adventures with gusto and verve. He called himself a monster ironically, because he wrote to reveal sexual predilections others strove to conceal at all costs. We're all like this, he was saying. My wealth enables me to tell the truth.

She called his hotel, spoke with his secretary, and made an appointment to see him that evening. Then she spent the afternoon sketching out the campaign that she would take to him.

When she left work, she decided to walk from her building down Broadway to his posh new hotel.

She was met at the door of his suite by a stylishly older dressed Frenchwoman with sharp black terrier eyes and the officious manner of a gatekeeper. "Olivier is napping," she said. "You will wait, *s'il vous plait?*" She withdrew.

Katherine occupied herself while she waited by inspecting the riotous profusion of flowers and plants de Carlo had filled the living room of the suite with. She stepped out onto the wide balcony to enjoy the view of the city, wondering if de Carlo would be as interesting as his book, or just another ego in search of applause.

Then he was standing behind her, wearing a red silk robe, his hands jammed into its pockets. His short, iron grey hair was still damp from a shower. He looked like Balthus's portrait of Andre Derain, she thought, with his popped, intense eyes, jowls, square head, and deep Riviera tan. His body was stocky, his shoulders massive, his stance like a boxer's, which he'd once been. His presence was electric with sexual power.

"Do you speak French?" he asked, his accent slightly cracked, and charming for that.

"Not well enough," she confessed.

"*Tant pis.* Very well, then. I must struggle with my English. Let me say first, please, that you are beautiful. That makes me happy."

Despite herself, she was flattered. "Thank you."

He gestured at the streets below and up at the towers of light. "I want everyone to read my book. Do you agree?" He regarded her with frank appraisal. There was something reptilian, even saurian, in his heavy-lidded gaze. It was bold, and hungry.

"That's my job."

"I need it to be more than your job, *ma cherie*."

"I can assure you, Mr. de Carlo, that GCI is totally committed to *My Life as a Monster*. The size of your advance guarantees that."

"*Bien sur*. That's why I asked for it."

"Although from what I've read in your memoir, you don't need the money."

He frowned dismissively. "You don't look like the type of woman who is easily impressed. I'm pleased by that."

There was an aristocratic *hauteur* in his tone that Katherine found herself responding to. He was sleek, virile, and polished by the rewards of an unrestricted life, but there was something else in his expression that hinted at an underlying cruelty. A cruelty that he had written of in his book as one of his many sides.

His secretary entered the room. He became a host, escorting Katherine with a hand on her arm to a sofa.

"Sit down, please. Would you like a drink?"

She agreed to a brandy, and the secretary left. He sat on a sofa across from her and focused his attention on her. He was openly staring at her breasts.

"If you have read my book, then you must realize that my motivation for publishing it is not financial. It is sexual. That should be clear between us."

"Well, I know you talk about the lovers you've had. A lot."

He shrugged. "But my purpose is not to brag of my conquests. I tell those stories because they were the most important experiences of my life. Everything that I have done, I have done with an erotic motivation. It may not be apparent at first, but it's always there—on the other side of the door."

"You should be a great success with the media, then."

"But they are all so stupid! Will you help me with them?"

Even across the room, he exuded an animal magnetism that brought the weekend to mind, and she blushed. Maybe, she thought, once you move into the sexual dimension, you can't get out.

Their brandies came. The secretary looked pointedly at her, and she pressed her knees together reflexively.

"Since I have been an adolescent," he was saying, "I have felt myself different from others. Why? Because I decided at that time—so long ago, alas—that sex was the only thing important in life, until death comes along. Sex drives me, as it does everyone, but I am honest about it. *I proclaim it.*"

He regarded her with such naked, impersonal lust that she was forced to look away.

10

"And then what happened?" he asked, breathing the question in her ear while his fingers busied themselves between her legs. She was feeling too sensuous to talk, but there was something insistent in his voice, in his need to know, and she didn't want to disappoint him. She was so glad he'd come back.

"He had this tremendous hard-on under his robe."

"What do you mean, tremendous? Like mine?"

"No, nothing's like yours. Bigger than average, that's all." She was holding his shaft in her hand, her fingers contracting around it.

"Did he say anything? Or did he just show it to you?"

"He just stood up, holding his brandy glass, and his robe fell open. It was just sticking out."

"What did it look like?"

"Oh, it's hard to remember the details." *Actually*, she thought, *I can remember every little detail. But I don't think you want to hear.*

He had three fingers up inside her, working them hard. She clamped her thighs tight over his hand. "Why don't you just fuck me, that's what I want you to do."

"Tell me. Tell me everything. Then I'll fuck you."

"It's a long story. You've got to let me tell it my way."

11

Listen to me. I must sound like a real slut, talking like this. But it's turning me on, too, remembering it for you.

You have to understand, it's like I've walked into a parallel universe, where everything is upside down. I feel like I'm becoming someone else. Everything is sexualized, and you know what? It's a lot more interesting seeing it that way, although sometimes it feels . . . dirty. I can't help that.

No, let me tell you about him my own way. Just a little, at least. Let me tell you why I just sat there and stared when Olivier exposed himself to me, why I wasn't outraged. Before you came along, I would have been—you know, what an insult to my professionalism! I might have even screamed sexual harassment.

I suppose it could have been taken that way, but I just felt flattered. Does that make me a slut?

I think Olivier is like you. He's old, and he's rich, but sex is all that's on his mind. It's like he's done everything else, and this is the level he wants to operate on because he finds it the most challenging. And he doesn't waste time.

Okay, I'll tell you. He does have a nice-looking prick, with a big head on it, like a walnut. But he only has one ball, if that makes you feel better. He's built like a bull. He even smells like one. He fucking oozes testosterone. I was so turned on, I was shivering. It was like I had a sex chart pinned on me, and he could read it as easily as reading a menu. I felt like I'd do whatever he wanted me to do. It was crazy, how much control he had over the situation—and we'd just met. First I meet you, then he comes along. It must be in the stars. I should take up astrology.

Ow, that hurts a little. I don't think I can take it yet. Play with me some more. Yeah. My asshole . . . Do *that* some more!

God, you're getting hard. This thing will be in a museum some day. No, you won't be dead. It'll be a living exhibit, like those butterflies. Oh, that reminds me, when we were talking, just before he showed it to me, he said he'd been to see the butterfly show. Can you believe that?

What was I thinking? I thought he probably wanted me to suck it, and I was having a problem with that. I mean, it's not like I wouldn't have. Like you said, I've sucked a few miles of dick. I've got the jaw for it. But I told myself I wasn't going to. If I couldn't do you, I wasn't going to do anybody else.

No, that's how I felt. But anyway, he didn't want me to suck it. He wanted me to watch, while he talked about what he was trying to say in his book. It was hot, just watching him. He's got these lidded, puffy eyes that he kept on me. We were mirrors for each other. I didn't pay any attention to what he was saying. No, it wasn't dirty. It was just ideas. Then she came into the room— the secretary. Her name is Eulalie—that's what he called her. That made him stop. I thought she had some kind of control over him, but maybe not. Maybe he's just got her programmed. He said something in French to her that I didn't get, and she left, but it was like he was waiting. But he didn't say anything more, and he was getting a little limp, you know?

She came back with a hand towel and a bowl of water and put it down on the table between us, and I could tell they both expected me to say something. I didn't know what he wanted.

I guess I figured that the best thing to do was just to keep talking about his book and pretend that his thing wasn't sticking up there.

Do that some more. You're on the right spot. Just—

All right. Here's what happened. He stood there and kept on talking, waving his hands around—he doesn't act French, more like an Italian—and Eulalie got down on her knees and—she didn't do what I thought she would. She soaked that hand towel in the water and began washing his feet. I mean, she cleaned every little piggy. Then she kissed each one. I couldn't see that very clearly, because she has long hair, and it covered his feet as she did it. But then she kept on washing him. Soaking the towel, and washing his cock and ball and his ass. She must have been scratching him as she did it, because he was getting red.

No. He stopped talking. He was watching what she was doing.

Then she started hitting him with it. It was like he had given her a signal I didn't see, and then she was whipping him with that wet towel. Yes—on his cock and ball! Hard! It must have hurt like hell, but he didn't make a sound. He bent forward a little—it *must* have hurt—but she beat him with that wet towel like she was trying to drive the devil out of him.

Yes, you know what happened. It just turned him on.

His eyes bulged, and he came—I mean, he just came really hard—and you know what? She caught it, or most of it anyway, in his brandy glass. She held it just right. Some of it got on her blouse, but she got most of it. She's good.

How did you know that? That is what she did. It is. She drank it straight down. There was a little brandy left in the glass, so it was colored. I'll never forget that—colored come.

12

She talks, and I listen, because I want it that way. It turns me on, listening to the dirty details. But I also know that's the best policy with women: if you want to fuck them, you've got to be patient and let them talk.

So that's lesson number one: listen. Most men don't get it. They want to do all the talking, which gives women time to figure out why they really don't want to have sex, after all.

Most men want to run things. They want to prove they're big deals. I could care less. All I want to do is run myself, which is enough ambition for me. I'd rather be between the sheets. Everything else is roles and masks and games, like Star says.

It all depends on what you want out of life.

At first, with a new woman, I just made believe that I was listening. But after awhile, I got hooked on it. It got me hot, voyeur that I am. I thought for awhile I might learn how they think, but because I listen to Kat doesn't mean I kid myself that I know anything about her. I just wait for cues, and play the role she wants me to play. Still, I want to hear everything, even though it takes time. Whole days and nights, when I get lucky.

I've got the time, because sex is all I do. When sex is everything to you, it becomes a calling, like any other calling.

13

My stories turn him on. He says that my willingness to share these secrets prove that I belong to him. Although he wouldn't understand the reference, I have become his erotic Scheherazade.

His ear is wet with my salacious stories. We lie in my bed and play with each other while I whisper the details of my erotic history. Each story is repeated, broken down, stretched out, and at last truly remembered. His encouragement stimulates me to a new understanding of what is truly erotic. It's more complicated—and much more exciting.

He insists on hearing the smallest, most graphic details—fingernails clean or dirty, unusual sounds at orgasm, my exact physical responses, the small talk afterwards—so that he can imagine the experience in his own terms. There are a few things he has forbidden me to do with my lovers, reserving them for us. I obey, because the little that is forbidden binds us. (One of these exceptions is that I must not wear surgical gloves with anyone but him. Another is that although I may suck, I must not drink any ejaculate but his.)

I've stimulated his lust with tales of men seduced in

all kinds of situations, with a variety of motivations. I've confessed to a kind of promiscuity women don't confess readily; it is an impersonal horniness, a powerful drive for satisfaction in anonymous sex. He knows that my needs are as strong as his.

This is why his part of our bargain is that he will not reveal anything about his past to me. He is to have no name, no past, no quirk of personality I don't observe for myself during our encounters. He is to be my invention. Our connection is purely sexual. I don't think enough of the male sex to want more.

Ours will be an honest relationship, in which I retain the upper hand. Most men are, after all, so sexually needy, so easily manipulated by any woman willing to use her powers, that they are contemptible. I don't think he's any different.

They don't know what they're missing sexually, because they are led by the sexual organ between their legs rather than the one between their ears.

I'm lucky to have been given an attractive body and a good mind. Notice that I put body first, because the world does; but it is possible to transcend biology. Without qualities of mind and heart and will, none of this would be happening. I would not be telling my intimate stories to this stranger, and he would not be giving me everything I want from a man.

Libido, I believe, is incapable of expressing itself fully without intelligence and imagination to guide it. Men may yearn for my body because it attracts them, but once they touch it, I can control them with my mind, and use them to fulfill my own desires. Theirs are irrelevant.

Not that I am unwilling to learn from him. His obsession with sex is so honest, his dedication to it is so unapologetic, that I am constantly being amazed. He is the only man I've ever known who seems to follow his nature unresistingly, without seeing anything wrong with where that might lead. This gives him enormous personal power, and power is what I want to learn about. So far, he's taught me that it involves pleasure and pain flowing into each other, according to the vagaries of need and attraction, dominance and submission.

I don't know where our affair will take us, but for now I submit to him with pleasure.

14

My penis made me do it.

Whenever anybody asks how I became who I am, Buddy Tate and no one else, that's what I say. Even in the courtroom that takes over my head sometimes, that's my plea, that's why I fucked up.

The jury never buys this, even though I'm telling the truth.

It runs in the family, I say. That's the way I grew up. We lived on the edge, Daddy and me, going around the West to whatever hole came next. He seriously didn't care about anything in life except getting off, and I guess I take after him. He set an example, you could say that; I watched him up close for years—sometimes through a peephole—and I learned secrets I share with women.

When I got my first stiff, my path was marked out for me. I didn't know anything about anything except that I wanted to get laid, say thank you ma' am, and get laid again. Like everyone, I started my sexual career jerking off. But that was short of what I needed, so I went to a whore for a meeting with the real thing. I enjoyed the introduction, of course, but not the arrest.

The court that sentenced me for such vicious behavior

sent me to a Sexual Misbehavior Clinic for a sex cure. The treatment was that you got to look at more porn than you wanted, and jerk off much more than you needed. Aversion therapy, is what they call it. When they turned me loose I was a recovered sex addict, so I took off for San Francisco because another averted pervert told me there were strip joints and beaucoup good scenes there.

I found the scenes, all right. Fine times, in the rear-view mirror. Then I met Robin, and we had what we had, we did what we did, and I lost her. I've been looking for her ever since, because she took something from me.

She became part of me against my will, and then ran off.

15

It was cold in New York, if only when contrasted with the warm Mediterranean and Caribbean ports where he usually wintered. Everywhere he went, Olivier had to keep the collar of his cashmere topcoat turned up. The wind sliced at his neck when he crossed a sidewalk between his car and the warmth of a lobby. He was dutifully following the itinerary Katherine had planned for him through Manhattan's media maze, but it made him grouchy and disdainful.

It was the people he met, he complained to Eulalie. From real estate developers to television anchors to Wall Street brokers, they all wanted to talk about money. No matter how much they had, they wanted his advice on how to make more.

No one wanted to talk about sex, other than as front page scandal mongering—unless it was to ask him about some Hollywood bimbo he'd spent a weekend with twenty years ago.

He was sitting in a hot bath in his hotel suite, at the end of a long day of interviews about the launching of *My Life as a Monster*. Eulalie sat on a stool, scrubbing him with a loofah. She had removed her starched white blouse along with her glasses, and wrapped a towel around her hair. Sweat gleamed between her pendulous breasts.

"Money, that's all they think of asking me about," he told her as she massaged his neck. "I feel like poor old Onassis. All you want, in the late prime of your life, is to catch up on all the pleasure you missed, but they won't let you."

"As you say, the book will be out next week. Surely you've done your best here. We can leave. We can return to the warmer corners of the world." They spoke intimately, in French.

He rolled his massive shoulders, indicating that she should work on the stiff muscles of his neck. Her touch was muscular and exact, the pressure she exerted with her fingers just right. She anticipated every need.

"There must be something I can do to change the focus. People who buy my book for financial advice will be very disappointed, I'm afraid. I'd be so much happier if they bought it for the good bits."

Eulalie had been Olivier's factotum for eight years because she was intelligent, amoral, and infinitely flexible. She had outlasted two wives and three mistresses—although Miranda, the current one, was proving difficult to shake off. She remained in Olivier's house in Tobago, waiting for his return, and sleeping with every fisherman on the beach. Now Eulalie had an idea. It would accomplish, perhaps, two ends at once, and she always preferred economy in her intrigues. They would fly down to the house in Tobago, putting Miranda on the spot as hostess, and they would invite this publicist to bring along whomever she wished, who might promote the book correctly.

She explained it to her darling as she soaped his front, scrubbed him, and prepared to shave him. Olivier was proud of his muscular torso. He'd been a boxer in his day, and he still worked out in the gym. But he didn't like hair on his body anywhere but on his head. He was a sleek bull seal, not an old bear, he said. So Eulalie shaved his body once a week when she bathed him, using an old fashioned straight razor to whisk away gray chest hairs, and then a safety razor as he stood up in the bath. It was exacting work, and she loved its closeness to danger. He trusted her with his life, and she had never failed him. Her hand was steady.

"Do you think that is the right thing to do? I would like to get away from this cold city. Do you think Katherine would come?"

"I don't think she'll have any choice."

"But what will Miranda say?" The thought of losing his jealous young American mistress with the bitter eyes disturbed him. She was extremely inventive, and even more brutal than he was.

"Miranda? Oh, I think she'll cope. Who knows? She might even like Katherine."

He chuckled, and it turned into a laugh that boomed off the tiles. "Maybe we'll all play my maze game. Maybe this time I'll have the right cast of characters, and we can really play."

The Maze? Eulalie suddenly felt a crawling sensation in her stomach. Her fingers contracted slightly in reaction to seeing her idea backfire on her. Blood flowed from a cut in his leg above the knee. It was superficial, but it was the first time it had happened. She hoped it wasn't a bad omen.

She moved quickly to stanch the flow with a towel, eyes wet at the thought that she might really have hurt him. But he stood before her unperturbed. The accident had stimulated an erection, and he always felt good when he got hard. He had spent his life looking for situations and women to challenge his potency, and here was one dropped in his lap, so to speak, by accident. Blood was always an aphrodisiac, but cutting?

They both looked admiringly at his imperious prick. Nothing had been too good for it, or too much, and now it wanted his own blood. It was a discovery.

"Do you want my mouth?" she asked solicitously, still pressing a towel to the cut she had inflicted on him.

He thought about it. What would be most pleasurable? How best to take advantage of this unanticipated gift of Priapus? Should he allow his faithful Eulalie to finish him off, or should he try to stretch his enjoyment by asking her to whip him?

"No. Something different this time. Play with it a little—just a little—while I decide."

She held his hardness in her hands and gently caressed its familiar lines, hoping he would change his mind and let her use her lips and tongue and fingers as she had so many times before. She wanted to ease her guilt.

"Tickle me," he at last commanded Eulalie. "Use your great long fingernails and tickle me."

"I don't know how," she apologized with a blush. She would do anything. But tickling? She wondered how touching him that way would serve to make him discharge.

"Eulalie!" he said harshly to her. "Were you never a child?"

"Bien sur."

"Then," he roared, "if you were tickled as a child as I was—until I wet my pants—you know how erotic it might be."

Although the gift of laughter had not been given to Eulalie, she was determined not to fail Olivier. She would strive to satisfy his new whim as she did all others.

She raked her nails tentatively down his thighs, then back up over his hard medicine ball belly, and over to his ribs, looking for places where he might be ticklish.

He waited expectantly, looking anxiously at his erection all the while. *The woman had no imagination!* he grumped to himself. "Hurry up!" He didn't want to lose this beautiful spontaneous growth. How many more of them would he have?

But then he smiled. Not because of the irony of the situation, for despite his wit, he was not really an ironist; but because it was working. He was relaxing. His nerves were dancing where her nails lightly played. Little stars of sensation began to form into a risible network, and giggles followed. Giggles, then guffaws, loud ones, amplified by the tiles of the bathroom.

It was unfamiliar at first, this forced humor that now rose from every point touched by Eulalie's nails; Some devastating frisson, an unbearable brush with what could not be stood. He saw himself stopping Eulalie in her exploration of tickling, but he could not. He was helpless as he laughed, like the laughing clowns in the circus, horrible and wonderful too.

It was as good as being whipped, he thought.

When he came, it was uncontrollable, like peeing in his pants.

16

I'll keep my own record, so that when this affair is over, I'll be able to look into it for clues to what happened between us.

It has been months, and I still don't know what to expect of him. My "education" has progressed, and I've been able to keep up with him, but he continues to surprise me.

Our weekends together have brought us closer than I've ever been with anyone, including my mother, and yet I do not know—at my request, of course—any scrap of information about his past, and I still can't predict what he'll do next in any area. I know that religion stirs deep animosity in him, and that he really thinks he's known me in another life.

That's about it. His sexual preferences keep changing, he varies his daily rhythms, and his habits seem to come and go. I don't think he's read much, but probably more than he lets on. There's some latent violence in him that extends beyond S-M play.

He's a light sleeper, he doesn't snore, and he wakes up ready to go. And go. So often that sometimes I wish he would just go, to give me some rest.

I was able to go down on him the last time we were together. I mean really make it sexy. He won't let himself come that way, though. He says he won't until I manage to give him deep throat. That's what he calls it, and I've picked up his language.

I don't think he's being deliberately crude only to shock me. It's not that he curses a lot. He doesn't emphasize his opinions with obscenities, but he talks sex talk when we're doing it, no matter how vulgar it is. I've never seen a man so comfortable with his sexuality.

He's always turned on, I think.

What has he learned about me? Just about everything. I talk to him and he listens. He listens when I tell him about me—how I grew up, school, early misbehavior— and he listens when I tell him sex stories.

What he thinks of me, I don't know. When he talks, I do what he says. I feel at peace, like he'll take care of everything. (Of course, in reality, he leaves and I go off to work to take care of things.) When I told him I had to go to Tobago for the company, and that I'd be staying at Oliver de Carlo's house on the beach, I thought he might get mad, or show some sign of jealousy that he couldn't go with me.

He'd been using a riding crop on my burning ass. He put it down when I told him about Tobago—we were talking, and he was just teasing me with it—and he got this distant look in his eyes.

"How long will you be gone?"

"Just a week, maybe a little longer."

"Well, there's plenty to do in this city. I might even look for a job." He was thoughtful.

Surprise. He wasn't concerned at all that I was going away. Yes, I was disappointed.

"Bring back some good stories," he said.

17

There comes a dark, cold day in every freelance pervert's life when he has to get out of bed, zip up his pants, pull on his boots, and go out and humiliate himself looking for a job. Star wasn't shy about letting me know that he didn't need company in the loft when he was working on paying skin, and my spending money was down to a wad of fives and ones and a handful of quarters.

When Kat took off, I had to face the inevitable. It was time to do the job walk.

Now, this is a problem for anyone in a new town, but just about impossible for a pervert on the run. I couldn't just walk into a temp agency and fill out an application. Not only do I lack office skills, I lack I.D. And since all kinds of pissed-off people are looking for me, it's hard to sit still, anyway.

On top of this, my attitude is bad—front and center, top to bottom. So when I left Star's loft that afternoon, I was King Kong on the trail of the necessary—get out of my way.

The sky was gray, the way it always is in New York. That's one of the reasons I started off thinking it wasn't my kind of town. After I escaped the boonies, I got used to warm and sunny California. I was used to some weirdness all night, and then sunny skies when I walked out in the late afternoon. I could be a laid-back lust dog.

On the sidewalk I headed north on foot, putting it in cruising gear and keeping my eyes open for opportunity. It was a Thursday in February, and the wind was blowing straight through me. The people I passed were poor Puerto Ricans and skinny yuppie kids in black. Everyone looked seriously depressed, which fit my mood. They were preoccupied, just getting through the day, like me usually. But today I was on a mission.

After walking about thirty blocks Uptown, my resolve began to weaken. I came to a park and sat down on a cold bench as the sun went down. Between the usual courtroom dialogue going on in my head and the fact that I didn't have a clue where to look for a job in New York, I began to feel the fear that hits me sometimes when I think I'll never find Robin. I sat there getting cold but unable to move, wondering if I'd caught some New York disease.

If I had, I had company on the benches around me. It looked like there were a lot of guys in New York who couldn't find jobs. They looked frozen in position, dead already, with snot still dripping from their noses.

I was tired of being on the run, tired of looking over my shoulder, tired of searching for a ghost. The voices in my head were saying things I had heard a thousand times, making my lips form words so that I was babbling to myself.

Just then a guy with a job came along, and I was rescued. He was a ratty little guy wearing two coats who was passing out flyers to the frozen mooks on the benches around me. Most of them threw theirs on the ground, but I read mine and laughed.

- FULL BODY MASSAGE PARLOR
- BEAUTIFUL GIRLS!
- GENEROUS GENTLEMEN INVITED!

I jumped off that bench like a fire had been set under me.

The flyer gave an address on a side street not far from the Empire State Building. I pressed a buzzer on the street door, and it was buzzed open. I walked down a corridor and got into an open elevator. The doors closed, and I went up to the Paradise Massage Parlor.

The doors opened, and the first thing I saw was a tall woman with blonde hair, big eyes, big red lips and big breasts. She sat behind a desk smiling up at me. It was the kind of smile a hooker gives you like spare change to a beggar—it didn't mean anything more than *hey, look me over.* But it had been a long, cold, discouraging walk from Star's loft, and I had the feeling that I had come home. I looked around and saw other women in the corridors off the reception area. I smelled familiar smells. Here was the world I belonged in.

''Your pleasure is our business,'' she said. She didn't say it like she meant it, but that didn't make the slightest difference to me. I could see that she didn't think much of my prospects. It looked like she had x-ray vision when it came to wallets, but that all cocks were the same to her. It hurts a man to have to think that way, but it's easy to get over. It was a business, like she said, and it was one I wanted to be part of, I knew that right there.

18

Olivier flew us down to the Robinson Crusoe island of Tobago in his private jet—just the three of us, our luggage, and a few cases of champagne from one of his vineyards. Everything else required for a week-long party was already on hand at his beach house. I thought he was crazy to think that lavishing a tropical vacation on what he called "media opinion makers" would change the reception for his book, but he lived by his hunches—and hey, it had worked for him. My role was to keep his guests pointed in the direction he wanted them to look in, and his role was to play gracious host. I suspected that he would attempt to demonstrate his ideas to them, one way or another. He was on a mission, in *My Life as a Monster*, to use his own life as an illustration for his sexual philosophy. I wished him well.

I was prepared to have some fun, prepared to do my duty for GCI, and come home to a promotion. I was even looking forward to whatever kinkiness Olivier could dream up, because it would take the edge off missing my butterfly man.

What I didn't count on was falling in love with Miranda. (There it is, that television word 'love,'' but I've written it in indelible ink on acid-free paper.) I think that it was some version of love that I felt for Olivier's wife the first time I met her, after we landed at Crown Point Airport. She was standing on stairs leading to the airport reception area as Olivier landed the plane. He pointed her out to me—a dim speck, waving.

When we stepped onto the airport tarmac, the heat hit me just as it had in the vivarium in the museum, but I saw no blue butterflies, only Miranda running toward us.

She is small and finely boned, and her hair is cropped like glossy black feathers. She wore white shorts, a bikini top, and a loose gauzy shirt from a good designer. Most people, when you meet them in such a way, are blurs whom you can later define for yourself. Miranda's self-definition was as clear as a seashell held up against a cerulean sky. Her dark eyes sparkled with what— knowing Olivier—I at first took as mischief. Later I realized it was pain I was looking at: pain she gave herself, pain she had given others, pain she yet had in store.

I shook her hand when Olivier introduced us, noticing how Eulalie, the faithful secretary, avoided eye contact with her. Olivier wrapped her in his big arms and picked her up off her feet, swinging her in the air. She was a butterfly too.

I could see she was one of those lucky people who are loved despite their certainty of being unloved, and it gave me an insight into Olivier. He didn't buy things, like the rich Eurotrash I usually met. He was like an artist carving a maiden out of ice. He spent his money and his time creating worlds of pleasure for himself and people to enjoy them with. He seemed pleased by my fascination with his wife.

It was hard to take my eyes off her as we were driven, in an old but well-maintained Mercedes, from the airport up to Olivier's beach house near a place called Arnos

Vale. I felt intoxicated by the warmth, the bright sunlight after New York's winter cold, the tropical smells and bird calls, and the liveliness of the people, but my gaze kept returning to her.

I watched her with Olivier. They sat in front with the driver, a charming black man who spoke English in a lilting patois. Eulalie sat silently next to me, her head turned away.

Miranda was cheerful but distant with him, obviously playing at being a dutiful wife. She assured him the house was ready for his guests. I could tell by her stiffness that she was holding herself back, perhaps because of me, but she didn't turn around.

Olivier, good host that he was, rambled on for my benefit about this island paradise. He loved its food.

"Do you like fish, Katherine? Best fish in the world here, I think. We get it fresh every day. The Atlantic, the Caribbean and the Gulf Stream all join here, which makes for excellent fish."

The house was superb. It sat on a bluff above the water, surrounded by exotic trees and flowers so bright they hurt the eyes. Roosters and goats walked about, freely grazing. I grew up with summers on Cape Cod, so I was prepared to open myself to the lush marine landscape; but this was overwhelming at first.

The house was large and cool. I liked best its wide veranda, and immediately removed my shoes to walk barefoot on the smooth terazzo floors. Servants greeted us with welcoming smiles, but I could only guess at what they said. Olivier was treated as a king returning to his palace. Eulalie went straight to the kitchen, to supervise preparations for dinner. It was plain she thought the staff needed strict Gallic supervision.

I was shown my room by Miranda, who said, "You must change into a bathing suit and go in the water with us. It's a tradition for all first timers to the island!''

Olivier and Miranda were waiting for me on the beach, and I was gratified by their obvious approval of the thong bikini I'd found at Saks before the trip. It was bright red, and minimal. I knew my ass looked great in it, but I thought Miranda was awesome, if only because she was topless, and her breasts—although not quite as large as mine—were perfectly sculptured. She wore piercings in her dark nipples. She ran into the water.

Then I noticed her back. It was covered with tattoos.

Like Neptune, Olivier led his maidens into the surf. The water was warm and silky, and I dived into it with the goal of scraping a New York winter off my skin. Olivier was protective.

''Watch out for sharp rocks and coral. Cuts don't heal well here. And the currents can be very strong.''

Miranda was further out, alone in an exercise routine of breaststroke and crawl. The waves lifted me and then slapped at my front, tearing off my top. I dove to grab it, and went back to shore to put it back on.

Olivier sank down in the sand beside me, staring politely as I fumbled with the top.

''Now you've been initiated, Katherine.''

''It's heavenly. I'm tingling all over.'' My nipples were hard.

''These media people of yours—do you think they will be able to stop talking about money down here?''

I didn't think so. But being in paradise might help.

Dinner was by candlelight on the veranda: sea bass in peanut sauce and yams, spicy rice, and a half dozen other dishes. Champagne, Carib beer and rum after dinner.

We walked down to the beach to enjoy the stars. In the distance I could hear the faint happy sound of steel drums over the pounding of the surf.

Olivier was feeling expansive. He was walking with his wife, pointing up to the stars, and Eulalie and I trailed behind, ignoring each other. The Milky Way spilled over the black sky.

He stopped, pointing to a giant sea turtle in the distance who had crawled ashore to lay its eggs in the sand.

"For thousands of years, these turtles have been coming to this island in March to lay their eggs," he told us. "They don't know why they do it, they just do it. They have to. Through sex, nature programs us all. We don't have any choice about what turns us on and why we do the things we do. We just feel desire, and we're helpless."

His hand dropped down Miranda's back to her ass and fondled it. I wasn't surprised by this indiscretion, but I was surprised by her reaction; she spun and slapped him. I could hear the *crack* her hand made against his cheek over the surf. Eulalie immediately sprung forward, to stand between Olivier and his wife, who looked prepared to strike out again. She was small but fierce-looking.

Eulalie said something in French, and Olivier replied in English: "Fuck you, my dear! Fuck you!" His genial expansiveness was no more. I saw in him the cruelty I had glimpsed in his hotel suite. His eyes bulged, and he struck Miranda with his open hand and she went down on her knees in the sand.

"Hey!" I think I yelled at him, and ran to help her to her feet. She was silent, but the expression on her face was as murderous as his had been.

I admit that I was frightened. I don't like such scenes. They illustrate, maybe, the primitive connection between sex and violence that lies beneath the sophisticated acting out of S-M. That's what Olivier said the next morning at breakfast, at least. But that evening, all I felt was shame for Miranda and him, and a desire to try to ease the pain she radiated.

I walked Miranda back to the house, waiting for her to say something. I found a piece of ice to put on her cheek, and she sat down on a hammock on the veranda.

"I'd better sleep out here tonight. If I went in there with him, I'd have to kick Eulalie out of bed, and then I'd cut his throat with a goddamned clam shell."

It was hard to sleep that night. There were mosquitoes and strange jungle noises above the incessant roar of the surf. I awakened in a sweat at dawn. The sun was hot.

After a tense breakfast, during which Olivier and Eulalie talked self-consciously about preparations for their guests from New York, Miranda surprised me by inviting me to drive with her to her favorite beach at Englishman's Bay. Olivier was obviously relieved that his wife would be out of his hair. The cook fixed us a picnic lunch, and we went off in the Mercedes.

On the way she made a detour off the bumpy, curving road and stopped at a huge, gnarled old tree. There was a bench near the great tree with an inscription from Hebrew on it: "There remaineth a rest. . . ."

We got out of the car and stood looking up at its thick branches.

"It's a silk cotton tree—hundreds and hundreds of years old. There's all kinds of stories about it."

"What kind of stories?"

"Black magic. I think the people who live here call it Obeah. Powerful juju, they say. Witches cast spells here, and witches have been hanged here."

We went back to the car. I noticed that she kept looking at her wristwatch. At last she started the engine, saying as if to herself, "Well, he knows where we'll be."

"Who?" I knew it couldn't be Olivier, that it must be a lover, and the tree was their rendezvous point.

"He's a fisherman," was all she would tell me.

Englishman's Bay was a delight: curving sandy beach, emerald green water, softly swelling waves. A tall bamboo forest clacked against itself in a steady sea breeze. There was no one around but lizards, so we went into the water without our tops. I tried not to stare at her tattooed back, but it was impossible. Snakes and dragons rose from the base of her spine into a luxuriant garden of twisted vines.

We lay on towels on the beach side by side, careful to stay in the shadows out of the direct sun.

"Have you ever been married?" she asked me.

"No."

"Why not?"

"I guess I don't see a lot of men I'd want to marry. Or that I'd even go to bed with, frankly."

"But you like dick, don't you?"

She turned her head to watch my reaction.

"Yummm. The right ones, that is."

"Hard to find."

"Well, Olivier certainly likes sex—from what I've read in his book, I mean." I looked away, diplomatically.

"Look, to be honest, I married him for his money. He knows that. I only fuck him when he begs."

From what I'd seen, I wasn't surprised, except by her coldness.

"I can make money. . . ." I began, my feminist ire rising.

"Not *his* money. Not *his* power. I needed him. So I married him."

"I still don't understand."

"He can protect me. I got into some bad trouble with my first. . . ."

She couldn't say the word. "Husband?"

"Well, let's just say we were married in our hearts."

"Did you love him?"

"I hate that word. But I guess I was obsessed by him. Then we just took it too far. . . ."

"What kind of trouble did you get into?"

Instead of answering, she sat up and pulled off her bikini bottoms. My eyes went to the puffy pink lips of her vagina. She smiled when she saw my fascination, but I knew she'd counted on it.

"I hope you like pussy, too."

It wasn't my first time with a woman—if you count my college roommate—but it was my first time on a beach in strong sunlight. It was my first time with a woman so openly sexual, and with whom I was falling so helplessly in love.

"I like *your* pussy," I told her, caressing her thighs, placing my hand over it.

"*Umm!* Stick your finger in me. I'd like that." She spread her legs to admit my hand, and I slid my index finger gently inside her. My other hand went to the tips of her breasts, playing with her nipple piercings. Her eyes glazed. She sucked in her lower lip, and I kissed it. Her mouth was small and eager.

I was conscious, as we kissed, that I was large and she was small and delicate—that I had to be careful with her, as with a doll. I always choose men big enough to make me feel breakable. Now I was the aggressor.

I bent over her to kiss her nipples, licking their hard tips through the metal rings, feeling the wetness start between my legs. My fingers were deep inside her, and she was rolling her hips and moaning softly. I heard her whisper, "Let me feel your tongue there, Katherine."

I knelt between her thighs, holding her vaginal lips open with two fingers to admire the glistening pink opening.

"It's so beautiful," I said. "I mean, you're so beautiful."

I imagined myself a man for an instant. No wonder men would do anything to touch, taste and penetrate such a delicious-looking fruit! Hers was the mirror image of my own, I thought. We're twins. Licking the stiff excited bud of her clitoris was like being able to lick my own for the first time.

I looked up and saw her pulling her nipple rings, then her thighs clamped over my ears, and she was jerking her hips spasmodically.

"You're getting me very hot. Very, very hot." I heard her say. "God, Katherine, I wish you could fuck me."

I was lost in what I was doing. Maybe I only imagined her words. But I wasn't imagining what I heard next: booming male laughter lifting over the noise of the surf.

I looked up. A tall male body was blocking out the sun. I could make out white teeth set in a great beard, but nothing more with the sun in my eyes. Neptune?

I sat up, squinting, holding my hand up to block the bright sunlight. Miranda sat up, too.

He was huge and dark brown, with long sun-bleached hair and a pirate's beard that spilled over his chest. He wore wet cut-offs with sandals. Not Neptune, but familiar.

"You've got a new playmate, Randy," he said.

He didn't recognize me. Out of context, he seemed both familiar and strange at the same time. The last time I'd seen him was in Manhattan, in my big bed.

"Redmon!"

"*Katherine*? What are you doing here?"

"This is too much," Miranda exclaimed. I didn't hear any jealousy in her voice, but there was a note of excitement. "I can't believe you two know each other."

I explained it to her and an impish grin showed me it was okay. She turned to him.

"Well, big Red, your timing is very good—except, where were you this morning? We waited for you at the silk cotton tree."

He looked properly chagrined. "Sleeping it off, to tell you the truth. Partied too much on the beach. We got into the rum."

"Where'd you come from just now?" I asked him, as if he'd emerged from my dreams.

He pointed. "My boat's out there beyond the reef. It's not much, but I don't need much down here. I knew I'd find you here, Randy, but—surprise!—you're with a naked lady. And one I happen to know."

As he spoke, he became more real—no longer an apparition summoned up by my overactive id, but a real man. I remembered how well he fucked me.

Miranda and I exchanged glances. I could tell we were thinking along the same lines.

"Well, I guess it's up to me," she said. "Get your pants off, Redmon. You're late."

He wasn't wearing underpants. He never did. I always say I hate jealousy, but I admit I felt jealous when I saw his half-stiff penis bobbing in the sea breeze. It had given me so much pleasure during our brief affair that I felt proprietary about it. I flashed on how it felt, driving into me.

But sex doesn't belong to anybody. Everybody belongs to it.

Politeness demanded that I let Miranda make the first move on Redmon. Down here, he was hers. But I had to swallow hard when she rose and knelt before him, licking his thighs and abdomen. I felt a tiny, sharp pang when she took his penis in her mouth. I knew where he liked pressure, where he liked to feel my teeth gently nipping his hard shaft. I knew he liked to have his testicles squeezed, and an index finger inserted in his ass.

But as Miranda's head bobbed, the jealousy I felt expanded to include her. Redmon's appearance had robbed us of the climax of our first embrace—and, I realized—she had planned it that way. Something told me that she knew he wouldn't be at the tree, that he would discover us as he did.

I didn't care. What ran through my head was, *he's mine*! This was quickly followed by *she's mine*! Mine, mine, mine. But they didn't belong to me. They belonged to themselves, and I could only possess them by making love to them.

Miranda surprised me by pulling away from him.

"I think you should do Katherine, Redmon. I want to see how you do it with someone else."

It felt so good when he entered me that I farted, but the surf covered the rude sound. My vaginal muscles caught and held him inside me and we started our horizontal dance. At first he was face to face with me and we kissed, but then he flipped me over and entered me from behind, pumping with an ever-increasing force that I withstood only by digging my knees and elbows into the hot sand. He was as good as I remembered, and I was as good with him. Miranda knelt beside us and stroked my hair and cheek, putting her fingers into my mouth for me to suck.

Then she whispered—the witch!—something in his ear and he pulled out of me, just as I could feel my orgasm start to build. But he left me hanging and moved to mount Miranda.

She was giving him her asshole, that secret chamber, and they were gasping with the effort of jamming his log into her.

My frustration added to my jealousy, I had never given him that.

It was as if I'd ceased to exist, as if I was losing them again. I could hear Miranda panting so as to ease his thrusts into her rectum, and her little yips of pleasure. I could hear, too, the cries of seabirds, but I didn't look away from them, because at last I saw that they were parts of an intricate mechanism that needed a third part. I could complete them.

I moved to Miranda's head and spread my thighs, and immediately she began sucking me with an enthusiasm that mirrored mine when I was sucking her. She forced a finger into my bottom—too roughly, I found out later, but I was beyond caring—and plumbed me as her tongue lashed against my clitoris. I watched Redmon's face as he pumped into her upturned ass, and he was laughing, his great head silhouetted against the cloudless blue sky.

19

When Redmon, with his sailor's eyes, saw people coming down the beach, we moved into the shade of the palm trees and put on our bathing suits. After the intensity of what we'd shared, we were separate again. I watched a lizard on a rock and it peered back at me, flickering its tiny tongue. No one spoke.

The picnic lunch was produced, and we sat on exposed, gnarly tree roots eating, watching the tide go out. I could sense Miranda closing up, as if she'd revealed too much of herself in the sand.

I made conversation with Redmon, hoping to draw her into it by being provocative, flirtatious.

"You timed that well. You must have smelled us."

He looked sheepishly in Miranda's direction, but her gaze was out to sea, where storm clouds were forming.

"Just lucky, I guess. But I might have known that the two of you would get together, if you were on the same island."

I teased him. "What do you mean? Do you think we're lesbians?"

"No. I thought I'd never meet a woman who liked to

make love as much as you did in New York, and then I came here and met Miranda.''

''You mean, we both know what we want?''

''Something like that. You could be sisters. Out there, I felt like you both were using me to complete a circuit between you.''

I saw Miranda's eyes flash. She was angry. ''You're full of shit, Redmon. I didn't need you, and Katherine didn't need you either. You happened to come along and we used you.''

''You knew I would come here, if I missed you at the tree. After I got up so late, I thought sailing here, not driving, would be the quickest.''

But Miranda would not be placated.

''I don't need any man. Not really.''

Obviously, Redmon had heard this before, and didn't find it any more persuasive than I did. It was just one of their arguments. Even the lizard seemed to be giving her a skeptical look.

''Why do you stay with Olivier then? Even after he hits you, you stay with the bastard.''

I could tell he was hooked on her, just the way I was. Jealousy is a bitch, but I felt it stab me again when I saw how emotionally involved he was with her.

''It's none of your business. Forbidden access. Keep out.'' She crossed her arms in front of her, as if keeping the intruder out.

It got to him. He threw up his hands. That was it. He wasn't going to argue with her.

''Well, all right, whatever. There's a storm coming up out there, and the tide's going out. I'm headed for my boat.''

Redmon knew how to make an exit. He stood up, looked from Miranda to me and back to her again. ''I'll be at the tree tomorrow. See you, Katherine.'' Then he was running down the beach to the water. I watched him swim to his boat, waiting for Miranda to say something.

"I bet he'll be there tomorrow, all right. But I won't."

"I like Redmon."

"Then *you* can meet him at the tree," she snapped at me. The look I gave her must have told that wasn't what I wanted. Redmon was Redmon. I realized that it was true, we had used him. It was our connection that mattered.

Now that he was gone, and there was no male buffer between us, we could talk like the sisters he said we were. It was like a hunger had come over us to declare who we were to each other. I thought of her as I'd seen her—in the airport, in the sea, in the sand—and each fleeting memory had some emotional meaning for me.

I couldn't take my eyes off her, like the lizard on the rock. I wanted to put my ear between her breasts and listen for her heart. Instead I offered to put oil on her sunburn.

"What about yours?" she asked, pointing to the backs of my thighs. So we rubbed oil on each other's bodies, hiding our nakedness behind a piece of deadwood, in a hole we'd scooped in the sand, well in the shade.

She stretched out prone in the sand and I knelt behind her to rub oil into her thighs and the globes of her ass. I couldn't take my eyes off the tattoo that covered most of her back, rising to her shoulders. I asked her to tell me about it.

"I got that in San Francisco at Asterion Studios. Star did it."

"It's like the jungle hides you," I told her, my fingers rubbing oil over the painting on her back. I felt her stiffen as I discovered the scar tissue under the tattoo.

"What happened?"

"My father burned me."

"Deliberately?" I was horrified.

"The son of a bitch wanted to chase the devil out of me." Her voice was muffled, but her bitterness was clear. Immediate.

"He must be awfully religious, in a sick kind of way."

"Do you know who Thomas Flood was? Ever heard of him?"

"Maybe. Television? He's a minister on television?"

"*He* burned me, and he did a lot worse."

"I'm sorry." She must have felt my tears drop on her back. She turned over, and pulled me down to her. We kissed for a long time, and then I rested my head on her breasts.

"*That*'s why I stay with Olivier. It's as simple as that: protection."

"From what? Who's after you? Is your father . . . ?"

A thunderclap made us jump, and then a tropical storm was coming down full force. We grabbed our things and ran for the car. The wind had picked up, and it knocked the bamboo trees together.

Miranda seemed excited by the storm. Her gestures became more dramatic. Her voice rose in pitch and she was suddenly expansive. She laughed at the quizzical expression on my face.

"I'm a woman with a past, Katherine. There have been a lot of men, but not many women. I do feel like we're sisters."

She steered the car confidently through the thick curtain of rain. The noise it made on the roof of the Mercedes was so loud we had to shout to be heard. She wanted to tell me what had happened. She was manic, banging her palms on the steering wheel.

"I love this weather!"

"Who's after you, Miranda?"

"The one I told you about back there."

"He must really love you."

"Till death did us part."

"But how can he be after you if he's dead?"

"Oh, he's not dead."

"I don't understand. Who's dead? Who's following you?"

"My father's dead. I bit off his dick."

My voice shut down to a whisper. "Oh, my God," I managed to croak out at last.

"That's what he said." Her voice was icicle-cold. "It's his goons I need Olivier to protect me from. The Christians."

At first I pretended to be shocked at what she'd done. I just stared at her, thinking, it's impossible to know who anyone really is, and it's probably best not to. But the truth was, I could still feel her scars under my fingertips. I was glad she'd done it.

The rain stopped just as abruptly as it had started, just before we arrived back at the beach house. I was quiet. There was a kind of fierce joy in Miranda's eyes.

On the open veranda the cook was sitting, shelling peas.

"Where's everyone?" Miranda asked her.

"Dat man be gone, child. He tek dat debbil Frenchie woman and dey go to airport. Boss had bidnis."

She handed Miranda a note, addressed to both of us.

"Darlings, I've been called to London. There's an emergency, and they need me. I'm sure you'll read all about it in the papers. Eulalie has canceled our party. (Sorry, Katherine—I throw good parties.) Well, we'll do it again, perhaps, but next time it'll just be us three."

There was a P.S. below his fat, trademark initial O:

"I'm sorry about what happened, Miranda." And then a P.P.S. below that: "Oh, Miranda, don't wear that sailor out. Naughty, naughty."

"The prick," Miranda said.

20

If your calling in life is sex, you can't go wrong in a massage parlor. Whatever happens, you're ahead.

Since all I had in my pocket was chump change, I decided to shoot for the moon and ask the blonde at the desk for a job. She laughed, and I felt like a kid applying for taster's work in a cookie factory. But that feeling passed as I stood there, because I wasn't a kid but a full-grown man. She could see that, so I didn't say anything more, just let her size me up.

It didn't take her long at all. Justine was the manager because she could take one look at someone and know what they were up to. She had to make decisions about the women who worked in the parlor and the guys who came to see them every other minute, all day long. She didn't make mistakes very often.

After she asked me a few questions, she knew we were on the same wavelength. Her house man had just been hauled off by immigration authorities that morning, and she didn't like doing business without a replacement. Timing is everything.

So in one lucky afternoon I found a job that I was born for. Being a house man meant that I kept track of what the women needed in their little cubicles, I mopped the floors, and I was available as muscle. I could be called upon if a customer was giving anyone trouble. I liked being a house man, the way the words sounded. It meant I took care of a house of women. The pay was all right but the access was my true reward.

I worked the evening shift, from when the garment center guys got off work and came for a rub down and a hand job from one of our "relaxation specialists" to the drunks who showed up after midnight. I was to keep things running smoothly, so Justine could keep the cubicles filled without a jam-up in the reception area. It was an efficient operation. Justine collected the parlor's fee, buzzed a free girl to come out and show herself off, and pretty soon the guy was on a table getting a rub down—and whatever else he could bargain for, handjob or blow job. Fucking was against parlor policy, but for an extra large tip some of the girls broke the rule.

Guys who looked Russian came by every night and left with bags, and I stayed out of their way. They were the owners, and sometimes they took a little out in trade. I didn't like that, because they were rough with the girls, and I had gotten to know each of them, one at a time. I didn't like to see one crying after a visit from one of the owners because she'd been manhandled or even raped, but there was nothing I could do in those cases.

The girls were all different. Six of them worked on my shift. Two were immigrants from Mexico and El Salvador, Rosa and Benita. They spoke Spanish to each other, had clients who spoke Spanish, and they were popular with black guys. Jade was Chinese, from the Philippines, and supported her family back home with her tips. Johnetta was a black college student. Marie was from West Virginia, a real coal miner's daughter.

But the one I went after first was Kyra. She was a

bottle blonde with a lisp, from Queens, whose eyes looked glazed with all the come she'd taken in. She called herself a nympho because she liked it too much. I figured she was just like me. There was no need to call herself names because others would do that.

Naturally, she was popular with the customers. After I set my sights on her, it was two days before she had a free half hour for me. But things were slow, late one evening, and she stuck her head out of her cubicle and smiled like a spider to a fly, Star would have said. A spider woman.

The odor of sex and disinfectant was so strong in her cubicle I had to breathe through my mouth. She was wearing a pink robe, so I couldn't see her body, but I knew it wasn't much. That wasn't what was sexy about her. It was those come-filled eyes and that creamy grin she gave me.

"I thought it was about time we got together," she said.

"You're right about that. Let's get down to it."

That's the way I could be in the parlor, not like with most women, not like with Katherine, who had to be seduced, no matter how much she wanted it. Just—let's get it on, dude.

She opened her robe and showed me her little boobs and a hairy black bush that came halfway up to her navel. I gawked at it, and she smiled proudly. It was quite a sight. There was a scar that ran from below her left tit into that jungle.

"What happened there?" I pointed to the scar. She pouted.

"Oh, that. Some guy got jealous."

Jealousy. I hated it almost as much as I hated seeing a cross hanging around a girl's neck—and Kyra had a gold one between her tits.

90

"Would you mind taking off that cross?" I asked her.

Her hand was already on my crotch, playing with the prize through my pants. Needless to say, she was good with her hands.

"It's my good luck charm," she protested.

"I'm superstitious," I told her, not wanting to go into it. She could understand that. Off came the cross.

"I've got some good luck for you right here," I said.

I unzipped and stepped out of my leather pants. There it was, about half hard, but hanging down. She was like a kid at Christmas with a new bike. She stuck her tongue out.

"Umm." That's all she said. Just licked her lips. It was the kind of reaction the big boy likes because he came to attention, fully erect.

She climbed on the massage table and sat there looking at me. She'd look at it, then look at me as if to see if I was kidding. She stuck her hand in her bush and pulled at it.

"I wish I had a camera," she said, spreading her legs wide. "Put that thing in me and fuck me to death with it. Don't stop until I say quit. Maybe not even then."

Her knees were up, and she was spreading her pussy with her fingers, parting the jungle so I could see her juicy pink. It was the right angle, at the right level. I got the head of it worked in and stopped, as I usually do, to give her time to get ready, but she was a pro. She took it all the way with one thrust, *wham*, rolling her hips as I started to move. It was something, to feel all that hair against my belly, like a bird's nest.

"Oh that is so fucking good, so fucking good," she was whimpering. I didn't think she was just giving me whore talk, because she was working too hard switching her tail around and snapping down on me. So I just let myself get lost in the sensations, squeezing her little boobs, sucking her dark hard nipples, and not bothering to kiss her because she was rolling her head back and forth too much.

"Give Kyra a ride!" she demanded. I thought she was delirious until I looked into those come-filled eyes of hers and knew what she wanted. I picked her up like a doll and supported her hips so she could move and up down like a toy monkey on a pole. Holding onto my shoulders, she moved so fast that I slipped out of her and she was just there in the air unconnected. I held her like that for a long minute, then penetrated her again, but this time in her asshole. I knew it was the wrong hole the minute I squeezed in, because it was so tight. She didn't seem to know the difference. I pushed half way in and it wouldn't go any further, so I stopped. I don't like to force anything—it's not in my nature. But she knew a trick. She could squeeze with her butt muscles so hard neither one of us had to move. Meanwhile, she reached down with her other hand and grabbed my balls, squeezing them just this side of pain. I started to pump into her and she sank her teeth into my shoulder, but I didn't feel it.

Afterwards, I had to sit down in a chair to get my breath. I'd put her back on her table, where she lay with her thighs open, my come oozing out onto the sheet. I could see both her holes peeping out under that black bush, red and pulsating, and I gloried in the sight. She was still coming as she lay there, still twitching.

I used a towel to clean myself off and got dressed. I had to get back to work, but it didn't seem friendly just to close the door behind me, and leave her there sizzling like bacon in a skillet. So I leaned down and rubbed my face in her bushy pubic hair, sliding my fingers into well lubricated holes, and her hips rose and fell, thump, thump, thump on the table.

After her shift was over I offered to walk her to the subway. It was one in the morning and cold, but she wore a miniskirt so short and tight you could see the crack in her ass from behind and get peeks at her bush from in front. She did have on a fur jacket for warmth, but it was like she was undressed from the waist down, clicking along in high heels. She was truly a credit to her sex.

She wanted to talk about my dick, and what she wanted to do with it, and of course I was happy she was thinking about the future. She wasn't smart, or deep, like Robin or Katherine, but I didn't think I was any better than she was. It was shop talk.

"I thought black guys were big. Sometimes I have to ask for a bigger tip because it's extra work to get them off, but at least I can make 'em happy. Size of that, I bet you don't get much head." She was sincerely concerned.

I thought of Star's slave Cyd, but I didn't want to discourage her from what she was about to say.

"I want to try it tomorrow. It's like a challenge, you know?"

"I could use a good blow job."

We were talking like this, not paying much attention to the street action around us, just being innocent, loony lust dogs, when we were stopped by a guy shouting into a microphone. I looked around and saw a young black guy in a black suit and a red bow-tie. He had a little gang around him, holding up signs. Christians—you couldn't get away from them. In their black suits, they looked like crows in the dim light.

"A woman dressed like that is a whore and a slut! Jesus! shield us from this temptation. Her body has the mark of Satan on it! The mark of the beast!" He was spitting venom.

And more like that, but I held my ears and walked on.

"Don't let them bother you. He came into the parlor last week—he's one of the big ones I was talking about. It was worth two hundred extra to him for me to polish his knob."

I had to laugh. Kyra was good for my soul, and I looked forward to keeping her as a fuck buddy. We were soul mates.

At the subway entrance it was awkward, saying goodnight to her. I realized I didn't know anything about her, except that she lived in Queens. Did she have a boyfriend? Kids? Did she go to school? We'd shared some quality time, but she was a mystery. Sex told me a lot about her, and I thought that was all I probably should know. My plate was full, with Katherine.

But I kissed her goodnight because it seemed like the friendly thing to do, and she looked sweet sixteen after her first date. She stood on tip-toe to whisper in my ear her goodbye:

"I never let anyone do my asshole before. You're the first."

21

Do you want to hear more?

You can feel how hard you've got me so far. I want to hear everything.

Well, (I continued) Miranda came to New York a week later, and moved into Olivier's suite at the Gibbons-Wakely. I couldn't wait to see her—I sent flowers to welcome her arrival, and billed them to the company. (After all, the sales of Olivier's book were strong.) She and Olivier would be reunited in a week, when I had scheduled bookstore signings for him, but the weekend was ahead. As soon as she unpacked, she came up here to see me.

She was more beautiful than she had been on our first meeting. It's all context, how you perceive beauty, but standing in the doorway of my apartment, she looked even better than she had in Tobago. Her silver piercings and deep tan were set off dramatically by the white fencing jacket that stretched tightly across her breasts, a faded denim skirt that I knew was from Gucci, and her shoes.

Let me tell you about those shoes. They were the same gold mules with the fake teardrop pearls from Manolo

Blahnik that I'd had my eye on for months. She was drop-dead gorgeous, but those are shoes. (You know they're one of my weak points—just short of addiction.) I just stared at them.

I told her I was drooling, and she laughed. She walked right to the bed, sat down, and took them off. She gave them to me to admire, and I held them up like champagne glasses. They were sexy.

"I love them because they make my feet look naked from the back. Are they too much, do you think?"

I smiled in recognition and led her to my closet door. I opened it ceremoniously, but I was giggling at the expression on her face.

"Do you think you're the one who's nuts? What you see before you is not just a collection of shoes, it's my life at least until recently."

You know what she saw: dozens and dozens of shoes arranged neatly on racks, open containers, in shoe bags, some even still in their original boxes. I've got pumps, sandals, boots, three-inch heels, stiletto heels—she dove for them, stroking their heel lines, holding them before her nose to savor the leather smell. In the past I've haunted shoe sales, which accounts for my treasures. I handed Miranda my purchases from the workshops of Blahnik, Clergerie and Sander, not to mention loot from Bergdorf's, Saks and Jimmy Choo's. She oohed and aahed over each selection.

When I handed her my latest favorite, a minimalist black sandal decorated with fake coral, she gave a little squeal, and it was like having an orgasm together. (All right, maybe I'm exaggerating just a bit, but I think we both left wet spots on the floor.) Girls will be girls. It's a fact, when it comes to shoes.

After that, she looked at my apartment. She really inspected it, and I observed her with that kind of nervousness I always feel when that happens. If they are people you want to impress, you hope they're pleased by your taste. If you're not sure how you feel about them, you feel exposed.

It spooked me when she looked at my crosses. I waited for her to make a comment, but she just examined them carefully as if she knew what she was looking at. Going up on tiptoe in her bare feet, she touched one and asked,

"It's fifteenth-century French, isn't it?"

She was right. I had found it in Paris, in my days as an art history major my junior year abroad.

"How did you know that?"

"It's something I studied, because of my father."

"For me, it started with my mother. She would give me one every Easter, when I was growing up. She said they were in memory of my father, who was a wayward soul we had lost."

"What happened to him?"

"He killed himself when I was eleven."

"Were you close to him?"

I had to think about my answer. "We were best buddies. He taught me a lot, I think."

"So your mother raised you?" She was wistful.

I was glad she seemed to have forgotten about the crosses, but we were getting into unexplored emotional territory. I saw what we shared, but how differently we'd been affected. We'd both lost fathers, but I loved mine, and she had hated hers enough to kill him—if that's true, that she did. She had lost a mother she loved, and I had been raised by a mother who tried to smother me—until I escaped. Her father was a religious nut, and so was my mother. As for the crosses, I had collected them because they comforted me. She rejected them because of her father.

We were opposites, we were twins. Sure that I was in love with her, I made much of our similarities and discounted our differences. But there were many of them. While my childhood had made me contrary, Miranda's had made her deeply angry, if not mad.

22

It was her.

I never thought that Kat would be the one to lead me to her, but I guess it made sense—a kind of whacky, birds-of-a-feather sort of sense. Everything's connected, if you look hard enough for the wires. Maybe we're interchangeable.

Miranda was Robin. When Kat told me the story of what she did in Tobago, I remembered how Robin had been before we'd had to run and hide—before the courtroom opened in my mind that judged us innocent one day, and guilty the next.

She was married to a rich man she wouldn't piss on, and Kat thought she was "in love" with her—so she had a claim on Robin, too. Me? Old Buddy was the past, tinkling along like a tin can tied to her tail wind—one she couldn't hear because it was so far behind. But now I'd caught up to her.

I knew Kat had some dynamite in her. It would just take time to light the fuse; it was buried so deep. But Robin—my Robin, with the bloody beak—she was a speeding torpedo, a depth charge. She ran on radioactive fuel.

When I told Star the news about Robin being back, he said that I was whacked, that I'd pumped my brains out in the massage parlor. He pointed to the blow.

"Have another line. You'll be seeing angels next. That'd be better for you, too."

I told him what Kat had told me while he played needle artist on Cyd's left buttock, as she lay prone on his table. Star could concentrate on his work and juggle three different conversations, while he was so stoned and drunk you wouldn't want to go for a spin with him.

"When's the happy reunion?"

"I don't know. Kat's involved, too."

"I think you're outnumbered, man."

"All I've got to do is out think them."

He snorted, as much to say that there wasn't much chance of that.

"Let me point out to you a simple, but amazing little known fact, Buddy."

"What's that?"

"Any woman over sixteen can out think any man who thinks with his dick."

"Lay off."

"They're a different species, I'm telling you. Isn't that right, Cyd?"

Her crooked eyes gleamed happily, backing him up. She winked at me. Thumbs up. What a crew.

"I've just got to figure things out. Then it'll be okay." By this time, Star had me half-convinced I wouldn't be likely to figure anything out that would work with them.

"Tell me this: does Kat know who you are, do you think?"

"No. She doesn't want to."

"That's what she says. Just wait till they gang up on you. My prognosis for this situation is that your days as a happy man are behind you, Buddy."

"Well, maybe, but you know how it is with Robin and me. We met at your studio, after all. You remember?"

"I've got total recall. She was there having her back done when you blundered in, wanting me to put a tat on your johnson. But I wouldn't go near such a weapon, if you'll remember."

23

Since we had to split up, all my dreams have been whacked-out nightmares. I'm never in control in them, because something is always happening that I can't stop, not even when it's me who needs the stopping. Robin's usually in them, of course, bare assed naked and crazy looking, with blood on her mouth that drips down her front until it covers her whole body. I'm just helpless—usually because I'm wrapped in some kind of cocoon that looks like it's made of chain links, but feels like silk—and Robin's standing over me with a whip.

The other part of the dream is in the courtroom. We're standing together with handcuffs on, gags over our mouths, and a judge is banging his gavel, only his gavel is a big heavy cross. *Boom!*

And then I see her daddy's eyes bulging when she did it. They're watching us as we fuck, as I slip the johnson to his sinful daughter. They're trying to warn me of something. Resurrection?

But all I wanted to do was see her. I woke up the next afternoon knowing that I had a mission. Before dark, I'd see Robin. Before dark, I'd kiss her bloody mouth.

When I got to work at the massage parlor that evening, Justine was waiting for me with bad news written on her face. I thought it was because Kyra had found out (I didn't hide anything—why should I?) that the black college student, Johnetta, was slipping me a little on the side. Johnetta was smart, and I liked talking to her about human sexual nature—in addition to being partial to any shady lady who could walk on my back and then turn me over and walk on my dick. Johnetta knew some nasty fucking tricks she was happy to teach me. She was a real acrobat.

But it wasn't jealousy that had gotten Justine upset. She was an ice queen, no matter what came up. With those Russians breathing up her skirt, Justine had to remain cool at all times. Cat fights were a daily occurrence—nothing she couldn't handle.

She told me that a man had been there, looking for me. He had said my name was Tate, and had given a good description of me. He wore a black suit, carried a brief case, and looked like a cop, but she could tell he wasn't because he didn't show any interest in the half-naked girls who peeked out at him when he yelled. She thought he was a Bible-thumper.

She told him to get lost when he wanted to know what time I came in. His response was to shout, "You are the whore of Babylon!" She said his eyes looked like a computer screen when he called her that. It made her nervous. Where was Babylon?

"What's up, Buddy?"

The policy in the massage parlor was not to ask any questions about anything except what's-your-pleasure, so I knew my job was on the line.

What could I say? It's the Christians—they're after me?

I'm willing to admit that I'm a few shy of a six-pack

—that being bent has driven me half-way around the bend—but I wasn't foolish enough to tell her the truth. I knew what it would sound like to her.

"It's somebody's husband, I guess," I shrugged. "A man of God."

"Are you sure that's all?"

I nodded. This was a story she could live with. She knew me. I'd been through the girls in the parlor and was still on the prowl.

"You can't keep it zipped, can you?" She winked, then eyed my crotch suspiciously. She'd surely heard about me from the girls, but she'd never shown any interest herself in the big boy.

After our talk I went about my work with half a mind. After giving it some thought, I guessed it was that black preacher who'd insulted Kyra on the street who might have steered Mr. Hopper, the avenging angel, to the parlor.

Mr. Hopper had been Robin's daddy's right-hand man. Once before he'd gotten his hands on me, and that wasn't an experience I wanted to repeat. I went to Kyra's cubicle to ask her about the preacher, but she had a customer.

Every cubicle in the parlor had a narrow closet-like area next to it where the house man could stand and check on the girl and her customer. I was supposed to do spot checks when I had time to make sure the girls weren't keeping more of their tips—they had to split with the house—than they should. It was one of the prerequisites of the job.

I like peeping just as much as hearing Kat's stories. It gets me hot because it adds to the variety of sex. Watching some strange guy get it on with a woman I've done makes me feel like I'm fucking her with his dick. Think about it.

I stuck my eye to the peephole and looked into Kyra's cubicle.

Kyra was squatting on her massage table, her big black bush positioned over her customer's open mouth. He was licking and sucking her while she played with his swollen prick. It stood up like a tower and there was a safety pin through the tip.

Ouch. I mean, *ouch!* My shank shriveled. I had seen plenty of ampallangs in the clubs and at play parties, but never a dick stuck by a giant safety pin. It looked like he'd just put it in, because blood drops were flying as Kyra expertly jerked him off.

It turned my stomach at first, I have to admit. Despite everything I've seen, there's always something new to get used to. Something that seems off the map at first, and then after awhile comes to seem as normal and natural as the missionary position. Who was I to begrudge how somebody else got off? He hadn't asked me to spy on him.

I made myself look through the peephole again. Kyra was standing next to the massage table, leaning over, feeding him her tit. He had the whole thing in his mouth, and from the look on Kyra's face—the come level rising in her eyes, to be exact—she was about to blast off. But she pulled it out (I actually heard a wet *pop*) and moved down to his waist, where she grabbed his dick and pressed it flat against his belly with one hand while she squeezed his balls with the other. She did it hard, because he was squealing, although not loud.

Kyra loved her work, and she put everything she had into each session. They talked a little and took a breather, and he bargained with her. She handed him his pants and he pulled out a wad of bills and peeled off two big ones for her.

I couldn't imagine what he wanted her to do next. I

didn't think she'd let him fuck her with that bloody safety pin, but she was a nympho—and the second part of that is maniac.

What she did got me stiff again. It was like someone had touched a live wire to my balls. Kyra turned her back on her customer and reached into a box on her dresser, where each girl kept towels, lubricants, oils, and condoms.

When she turned back around, she was pulling on a pair of white latex gloves. She snapped them tight, and I could feel my heart snap. I confess, I'm a latex glove freak. They were my first fixation, beginning the summer I turned eleven, when a beautiful nurse in a clinic had pulled a pair on to inspect my injured dick. I'd been masturbating so much I'd really rubbed it raw. When I showed it to Daddy, he threw me in the pickup.

Maybe it was the powdery rubber smell of the latex, or maybe it was the way the nurse snapped them on. Probably it was just that it was the first time a woman's hand ever touched me where it counted. She put Vaseline on it, and she was smiling to herself as she did it. I was big for my age.

Kyra played with her customer's tool for a little while, using KY Jelly to lubricate him, and then she made a fist and stuck it in his butt. She was slow and careful—the girl was a real pro—and as she fisted him she played with his balls, pulling the hairs so she stretched his scrotum. Maybe a half hour passed.

Her arm was in his ass up to the elbow when he reached down and unfastened the safety pin through his dickhead. *Whoosh*! He shot his sperm in a great liquid loop that landed on Kyra's titties. She withdrew her arm from his intestines, peeled the gloves off, washed her hands with antibacterial soap, and used a towel to clean him off. It had been a championship performance, and she looked tired.

He stood up with his back to me and put on his pants, coming up with that fat roll again to give her another big one. He was an older man, with a boxer's shoulders and neck, a deep tan, and gray hair cut short.

After he left, I went in to see Kyra and collect the house cut. I congratulated her on a job well done, and she handed over the money. She said she knew I was watching, and she wanted to give me a good show. I asked about her customer.

"I don't know. He's French, I think. Kinky, but nice."

"You are a credit to your sex, Kyra."

She laughed, pleased with my compliment. I guess she knew how good the show had been for me by the bulge in my pants.

"You tired after that?" I asked.

"I guess so. Why?" She knew what I had in mind, but she wanted me to ask. It was only fair.

"I haven't come yet today, and those latex gloves got me stiff as a poker."

I reached for her hand and placed it on my crotch so she could feel the effect her performance had had on me. She tickled it.

"You want me to try . . . ?" she asked, lowering her voice to a whisper, like this was a secret just between us, her trying to give me head. I nodded.

"Yes, Buddy. I want to. I want to, really. I think I can do it this time. But you got to kiss me first."

I kissed her, running my tongue around her teeth, and then deep kissing her, squeezing her titties as I did.

She fell to her knees and unzipped my pants. Holding my johnson with both hands, she opened wide. Her cheeks bulged with just the head, and I could feel her tongue flicking it. She was good, and I was losing myself in the sensation, heading down the road to glory, when Mr. Hopper's face zapped into my head. One minute I was getting a blow job from one of the best, and the next minute I was standing in a courtroom. The gavel banged down, and I was sentenced to impotence.

24

Robin was afraid. Fear kept her company, shadowed her, and in the end sustained her. It held her together in the absence of faith. The forms it took drove her actions and compensated for her lack of will.

Now it felt like the walls of the hotel suite were closing in on her. She had ordered Olivier's flowers removed when she arrived, but their heavy fragrance still lingered in the air. The walls were closing in, and she was suffocating.

She stepped out onto the balcony to escape, and looked out over Midtown Manhattan. Its massed light mocked her inner darkness, offering to fill it with whatever she chose. She trembled in the stiff late night breeze. There were too many choices. It was too late.

Automobiles were streaks of light on the streets and avenues. She held to the balcony railing and forced herself to look down at the canyon below. Vertigo made her draw back.

Things were spinning out of control, creating a vortex that she had to resist with all her precarious emotional balance.

Buddy was somewhere out there, she knew it, wandering in this canyon or that, looking for her. Somewhere out there, her father's avengers were looking for her, too. And somewhere out there, Olivier was moving towards her. He was on his way, Eulalie had informed her by telephone that morning. Of course, after Tobago, he would be unhappy with her. Perhaps his patience would be exhausted, and he would threaten her. He could be unpredictable and kind, or unpredictable and cruel, but he was always unpredictable.

What if he withdrew his shield of protection from her? How long would it be then before she was sucked into the vortex?

Now there was Katherine, to complicate matters further. She knew that Katherine thought she was in love, and this pleased her vanity; but it, too, frightened her. Katherine had no idea what she was getting into. She thought she was sophisticated, that she knew the world, that she could play without getting hurt. But she knew nothing.

She held her arms up to the night sky, but kept her slippered feet securely anchored in the balustrade. If she could find the courage to jump, she would be free, but only in her falling. At the bottom, before she escaped into oblivion, their hands would catch her. They would squeeze and pull her and reach into her insides for what was no longer there.

With Buddy, she had hoped that sex would help her escape. He was Priapus, a god pumping life into her; but even he could not fill her vacancy. With Olivier, it was money and power. What did she hope for with Katherine? Love?

She turned from the railing when she heard the buzzer, and went back inside.

25

When Robin opened the door, seeing her again crowded out everything else. The months of missing her, the betrayals, the blood, didn't matter.

She stared at me with the same look on her face she had the first time I saw her, like someone struck by lightning—cold and jagged and wild. I stepped a little closer, and I saw the familiar tiny scar on her chin that I always thought was spidery.

I didn't think she would close the door in my face, but I stepped inside, anyway, and pulled it to.

"It's been awhile," I said.

"How did you find me?"

"Kat told me where you were."

"God damn you, Buddy. Where have you been?"

"You made yourself hard to find."

"I was scared."

"I know." At one time, I remembered, I thought I could protect her—somehow help her feel less scared. You always think you can do something, but she was busted up inside way before I got to her.

I put my hands on her shoulders and leaned down to kiss her. I could feel her shaking, but she kissed back until she started crying, and I just held her. I'd thought I was mad at her, but I didn't remember any of that.

We sat on a couch and tried to talk. It wasn't easy, because there were a lot of topics we wanted to avoid. A lot of dead ends to be backed away from. She sighed the way she used to, and put her head in my lap.

"So you got married?"

"He asked. It seemed like the right thing to do at the time. He takes care of me."

It almost sounded like an apology, the way she said this. She was scared, that's what I heard.

"Katherine says you hate him."

"She should mind her own business."

"Well, she's got her eyes on you."

"I should take a firm hand with her, correction for loose lips."

"That's my job."

She smiled for the first time, and it gave me a little chill. We were on a familiar track, back with the games. She brushed away her tears, and her eyes got that struck-by-lightning look again. I guessed she was remembering how we used to fit together.

I played with her hair as we talked. There wasn't much of it, but I liked its silkiness. A woman's hair tells you a lot about her, just like her teeth. Robin's were small, even and white, and I got excited watching the way she ran the point of her tongue over them.

After awhile my hands went where they always went on her body. There'd been some changes. Her breasts were bigger and firmer than I remembered.

"You got implants?"

"They were a birthday gift from Olivier. He likes them bigger. I didn't care one way or another, so I went ahead and had them done."

"Oh."

I preferred her real titties. I didn't like to think she'd do so much for him. What else would I discover that she had changed for him?

"Buddy, they're just tits. 'More to hold onto,' he said."

My hand moved over her little flat belly under the robe.

"You've lost weight."

"I vomit a lot. Nervous stomach—I can't keep anything down."

"I think married life is killing you."

I rolled her clitoris like a wet marble between my fingers. Popped a finger into her tight pink, and followed it with two more, my little finger in her ass—the way I remembered she liked it when we were just fooling around. Her breathing picked up.

"You haven't lost your touch."

I guess she could feel me getting hard under her cheek. She sat up and unzipped my pants. The big boy had been shy with Kyra, but he remembered mama. I'm sure your body remembers things your mind has forgotten. The boss wasn't likely to forget her. It was like the sight of him standing at attention cheered her up.

"It's bigger than it was, Buddy. Isn't it bigger?" She was teasing.

"Well, it's all natural. Maybe it's been stretched."

"Let me suck."

"Just get it wet. I've waited months to fuck you."

We shucked our clothes. She licked and sucked and rubbed it over her face, and when it was ready she stood up on the couch over me and slowly lowered herself until her pussy brushed the head. She had always liked to tease me before she put it in her, before she sat in my lap, with its entire length inside her. It was how we used to sit and talk, face to face, hardly moving a muscle for hours—sweet, get acquainted sex time.

"Buddy?"

"Yeah?"

"What kind of games are you playing with Katherine?"

We had a rule, when we discovered this way of talking to each other, you could ask any question you wanted to, and the other person had to answer.

"Are you jealous?"

"I just want to know. She's not like us. You have to go slow."

"I'm going slow."

"Umm."

I was pinching her nipples to distract her. It was my business what I did with Kat.

"Have you done anything serious with her yet?"

"I make her tell me everything she does, every detail. I encourage her to do what she wants to do anyway. She tells me stories."

"And you get off on them?"

"Oh yeah. I do."

"How come you never wanted me to tell you stories?"

"Truth?"

"You've got to say the truth."

"I couldn't handle it. Not with you."

"But you can with her? You can hear about everything she does with someone and not be bothered?"

"That way I can control her. If I know what she does, I own her. It doesn't bother me."

"But you have to trust her."

"I don't trust anybody. But I don't think she'd lie. She's just getting into this."

"Stick your finger in there, like you used to."

She was breathing harder. I put my hand flat on her belly and pressed, trying to feel myself inside her. My finger was playing in her asshole.

"That's good," she told me. "Now I feel it. God, it's been so long. . . ."

"I've missed you, Robin. I've been looking for you for a long time. We weren't finished. . . ."

"I was hoping you'd find me."

"I never thought it would be Katherine who'd lead me to you."

"Why'd you pick her?"

"I looked for you in a lot of women. She turned up."

"But what do you want to do with her? You know what I'm talking about. Tell me."

"I want to turn her inside out. I want to take her into the zone."

The zone was what we'd called how close we got through pain.

"You want to make her like us."

"She is like us."

"Fuck me, Buddy, just like you used to. Let me ride the carousel."

It was what she called it when she moved her little body up and down, riding the pony, impaling herself again and again, faster and faster, until she was all motion, and we were perfect together just as I remembered it, just as it was meant to be.

I had closed my eyes and was just staying with her—wherever she wanted to go, however long she wanted, feeling connected again and lucky—when she stopped cold. When I opened my eyes, her face was turned away from me.

26

Olivier had let himself in quietly. He liked to sneak up on Miranda, hoping each time to discover something about her that she wouldn't show him knowingly. He stood for a long time in mesmerized shock, watching his wife impale herself on a greasy looking zero's enormous penis. As he spied, his pleasure grew.

Thinking, as he watched, I have no idea who she is. And him?

After his massage, he had driven himself—in the black 1962 Austin he used as his New York car—to the GCI building. There he sat with Katherine and planned his upcoming television and bookstore appearances. He looked forward to matching wits with the mediocre talking heads with whom he would be discussing his book. Having alleviated his fund's immediate crunch by selling certain overvalued stocks short, he had cleared the time to devote himself enthusiastically to the publicity campaign.

Wait till his interviewers heard what he had to say. There'd be screaming in the television control rooms.

The fisting in the massage parlor had made him feel good and vibrant. His fundament had been scoured, and now he was empty, waiting to be filled again. He looked good. Lurking in the shadows, he was a most elegant voyeur, in a tailored blue windowpane-check suit and his trademark long black silk scarf. He was ready to have it out with Miranda.

Now fate offered him this opportunity to confront her. He would say to her something like, *you've never given me what I married you for, what is in your power. You refuse to play the darkest games with me. You have never scorified and cleansed me.*

He was so gratified by the sight of his wife straddling the stranger that he could not stop himself from applauding her performance. He checked himself, but she froze like a wild animal hearing a noise. They *were* animals—naked and helpless, connected like two wild dogs caught in copulation.

He stepped into the light, smiling at them.

"Oh, don't bother to get up for me," he said.

They stared dumbly at him. Then Miranda blinked, as if to make him disappear, and blinked again.

"Surprised? But I told you I was coming, Miranda."

"You were spying on us."

"Guilty."

The zero spoke to him. "Her name is Robin."

"She's my wife, and she calls herself Miranda with me," he snapped, realizing immediately that her past had caught up with them.

He moved closer and reached to stroke Miranda's hair. She ducked to avoid his hand, but he was persistent. She was his, after all.

"This is Buddy Tate, Olivier. The one I did all that with, the one who's been looking for me."

"And now you've found her. This is a happy reunion."

Olivier hummed as he thought about this, reaching

down to grasp Miranda's breast. Her nipple was wet and hard. His hand moved up to caress her shoulder, his heavy-lidded eyes fixed thoughtfully on Buddy.

"I've heard many stories about you, Buddy, both bad and good. I thought probably I'd never meet you—that you would always just be a story my wife told me."

"I've heard a lot about you from Kat, so that makes us even," Buddy replied, as cool as if they were talking in a boardroom.

"Kat?" Olivier blinked. "You mean Katherine?"

Buddy nodded slowly. "I'm part of the family, Ollie."

His calculated insolence irritated Olivier, who was proud of his name. The news that he was fucking Katherine was intolerable.

"But you're nothing. Look at you—what do they see in you?"

"She told me you only had one ball, too. Sorry, but a family shouldn't have any secrets from each other."

The triumphant glare in Buddy's strange eyes was enough to make Olivier step back. He loosened his tie and sat on the sofa opposite them. He could taste his humiliation, and it was as sweet as it always was. But it was subtle, delicate; it had to be nursed along. He would not rush the denouement he hoped for.

He no longer cared to confront Miranda. Buddy had his full attention. He recalled some of the stories Miranda had told him about their adventures together, and Buddy grew in formidability.

The man was still hard, he noticed, when Miranda at last stood up and disengaged herself from him. He had been interrupted before he could ejaculate inside Miranda.

Still naked, Miranda sat on the sofa next to him, her full breasts bobbing slightly as she sank into the cushions. Buddy watched them both, waiting patiently for what came next.

"Now that he's found me, what are we going to do?"

"I think it's time to open our relationship a little wider, don't you? If I'm to share you, there's something I want. . . ."

She knew what he meant, if Buddy didn't. She shook her head. "I don't want to get into that."

He smiled. "You'll have Buddy to guide you in the right direction. He'll know what to do."

He removed his suit jacket, and began to untie his shoes.

"You know what he wants us to do, Buddy?"

"It looks like he wants a three way to me."

Then he took off his shirt, unzipped his trousers, and let them fall. His expensive suit lay in a heap on the rug, and he stood naked before them. Ready.

"He wants us to play with him. It's what he's been wanting from me, what I wouldn't give him. I told him I was through with it."

"Hell, let's just get out of here. Come with me."

"I can't."

"Why not?"

"Because of what he'd do."

Buddy didn't get it, so she had to tell him.

"All he has to do is pick up the phone, and they'll come after us with butterfly nets."

"You mean, he can sic the Christians on us?"

"And the law."

"That does put a twist on it, doesn't it?"

Buddy stood up, penis at half mast. He saw the situation, bang, and realized that, sure enough, he was trapped again.

"Well, I guess it's all in the family."

When it's inevitable, get right to it, was his motto.

They set to work. Olivier carried bags of toys with him wherever he went. Miranda brought them out and placed them in the center of the room. Buddy watched as she dressed her husband in his secret uniform. She laced a leather corset around his waist and pulled the laces tight, pulled his arms behind his back, and fastened his wrists with leather handcuffs. Forcing him to his knees, Buddy helped her pull a leather hood over his head that left only his mouth and nose exposed. When he shook his head because it frightened him to have his vision shuttered, Buddy slapped him lightly and he sank back down on his knees.

He was ready for the games. Since he could only imagine what they were doing—and he had a vivid imagination—every sound they made was magnified. He waited for the first blow, but it didn't come. He felt that they were near, and together, but they were paying no attention to him. They were whispering.

Then he was being picked up and put on his feet, and pushed across the carpet, stumbling, only to be caught by Buddy's strong arms. Then cold. Wind. They were taking him out on the balcony! He was pushed down and they left him.

Now he was truly frightened, and this feeling was accompanied by a delicious sensation in his penis.

He whimpered as he felt the first hot drop on his bare shoulder. The next fell on his bare buttocks, followed by a slow rain of pain. They were dripping hot candlewax on him, taking their time, letting the slow torture build.

But they stopped too soon. He was stiff as a sausage, and they stopped.

He cursed them. "*Amateurs!* You can't do that!"

He listened, waiting hopefully for them to continue— for the rain of fire to ignite his nerves, to shock his body into greater life. He could take much more; Miranda knew that he never got enough.

He couldn't anticipate their ingenuity. They undid his wrists and pulled his arms through the balustrade, cuffing them again so that he was positioned awkwardly with his head over the railing, and his buttocks in the air. He was suspended in space, held back from plummeting forty-six floors to the street below by the lacing of his corset, and leather cuffs.

The first slash of the crop was welcome. The second made him cry out. Buddy must be wielding the punishing leather, he thought. The blows that fell were heavier than she was capable of. He stopped counting after twenty, when his mind shut down and he was free at last, soaring on the updrafts, looking down at the bright world below. Finding in the darkness the light he sought.

They uncuffed him and pulled him back into the living room, but they weren't done. They were whispering again. He was conscious only of gratification. He had never felt so alive, triumphant.

They cuffed his hands behind his back again, tugging and pulling at him as they wrapped him in rope, making a cocoon for him. They finished by tying his black silk scarf around his neck.

What was this? He waited, but nothing further happened. He lay wrapped tightly in his bindings, as if entangled in a spider web, imagining that his torture would resume at any moment. The anticipation kept him hard. Sweet, delicious anticipation. . . .

Then Buddy sank down next to him on the sofa, and at last he spoke, in a low voice rough with passion.

"This is part of it, too. I want you to listen while Robin gives me head. She knows just how I like it. . . . Listen."

He could hear the sounds of fellatio, the wet slurping he was certain Miranda was exaggerating.

"No . . ."

"Why not? It's only fair. You interrupted us, earlier. Just be patient—we'll get back to you."

The soft sucking sounds went on and on until he heard Buddy shout his pleasure. It was as if they rested, then. He could hear them breathing together in ragged time like dogs, like animals, or playmates. God, they were good together!

He felt Miranda's hand on his sore penis and expected that she would take mercy and at least masturbate him to completion; but she pinched the glans and held his slit open with two fingers. She inserted a plastic straw into his urethra and pushed it slowly, carefully, inside. He arched his back as if to escape, but Buddy's hand was squeezing his testicle, pulling at it. He saw stars, and screamed, and came, at last fully scorified.

27

When Miranda showed up at my door she was a mess. Her face was puffy and her eyes were red. She was shaking when I hugged her, but she wanted to talk. I made camomile tea, and ran a bath for her, happy that she'd come to me.

"Buddy Tate is back," she said. "He found me."

"How?" I tried to show no emotion.

"Through you, sister, Through you."

She sighed and leaned back in the water, watching me make the connections. Nodding when she saw that I got it.

"It changes things, doesn't it?" she asked.

"How do you feel about him?"

"Just like I did. He's got his fingers in me. I can't get loose." It didn't look to me like she wanted to.

I turned my head and stared into the steamed-up mirror, looking for the right mask to put on.

"What happened?"

"Buddy surprised me—he likes to do that."

I knew that. Yes, I knew that. (*You son of a bitch!*) But I kept silent about what I thought.

"Well—what happened?"

"We were making love, and Olivier let himself in and was watching us. A real creep."

"Didn't you know he was coming?"

Eulalie had called her from my office to tell her exactly when he was to arrive, of course. But I didn't remind her of this, and I didn't expect an answer.

"Well, he got what he wanted."

"You did a scene with him?"

"I'd . . . put it a little more strongly. But he was happy. The pig. Everything we did to him, he wanted more. And Buddy just kept pushing it, like he always did."

I wondered if perhaps it wasn't Miranda who had done the pushing all along, but I didn't say that, either. The stranger I knew—at least, the one I invented—was capable of those games and even darker ones. But he could also be manipulated, I knew. Miranda was a mistress of manipulation.

We don't know anybody. People are who they need to be at the moment. When that moment's gone, they peel off one mask and show the next one. I didn't know Miranda any more than I knew the man who's found her: Buddy Tate. I made up the man I needed. It did change things to know his name and his history.

"It scares me," Miranda said.

I soaped her back, so I could study the curve of the snake that ran up her spine. I felt the scars hidden in the vines as I rinsed her. Whether she was truly helpless and frightened or simply mad, a feeling for her rose into my mouth that was almost physical—a swelling, a surge of tenderness, of protectiveness, I don't know what to call it, really. What came out of my mouth was this meaningless syllable, "love."

She reacted as if I'd slapped her.

"Stay out. The gate's closed, Katherine. You'd only get hurt. All I'm good for is the games."

I hated the name, but I spoke it: "And Buddy?"

She nodded. I handed her one of my robes, and she put it on.

"Maybe the games are about love."

"I don't think so. I think they're about being alone," she said.

We were sitting on my bed with tea, like proper ladies. "Love is an illusion. What comes out in the games is some kind of truth."

"What about Buddy, then?" I couldn't let go of it.

"What about him?"

"Do you think he loves you? Or me?"

"He doesn't know what that word means—just like me. We need each other, that's all."

"I need him, Miranda." I blurted out, surprising myself. While a hot bath and hot tea had helped to revive her, I was slipping into self-pity, and hated myself for it.

"Why did you tell him?" she asked. "Why?"

"It was part of our deal."

"You told him everything?"

"It got us both hot."

"He never asked for any stories from me. I wouldn't have told him, anyway. It's none of a man's business what I do with someone else."

"He thinks it proves he owns me, because I keep no secrets from him."

"Men like to think that."

"Being in control, you mean."

"Yes. Look at me, Katherine. First it was my father who did the controlling. Now it's Olivier, wanting to pull my strings. I'm a puppet."

I didn't buy Miranda's helplessness. I knew different. But her complaint gave me an idea of how to keep Buddy. There was one way we could share him—make him our puppet. She would know how to do it.

28

I knew that I'd lost Robin for good the night I found her. It was the way she pushed me to help her play with old Ollie. What we did together before he showed up didn't count, I saw that. Not next to what we did to him. Hearing him beg made her eyes shine.

But I was still hooked on her. Maybe too much time had passed, and she'd made herself a mask called Miranda by marrying a rich man, but she hadn't really changed. The games don't lie about the players. You can't escape your past. You do some things, and they're done for good—signed, sealed, and delivered. You have to pay.

He said that we could share her. However we wanted to work it out, he wasn't jealous. I was welcome, because together, we had given him a healthy dose of what he'd spent his life looking for. We'd be a family, he said. But she couldn't go off with me. He owned her, because of what we'd done to her daddy.

Star was right, as usual. She was a spider woman. When I told him about our scene with Ollie, he just gave me his evil laugh. Cyd giggled on cue.

"This guy sounds like a heavy hitter, Buddy. You're not in his league."

She might give me little pieces of herself. I could even find parts of her in other women, like Kat and Kyra. But I couldn't have her. It was the bare-assed truth, and I had to live with it.

I thought about what Star said on my way to work the next afternoon. No, I wasn't in Ollie's league. I'd been born a loser, and I'd probably die like one in some trailer park from hell, broke, and babbling. But in the meantime, as long as I could get the big boy revved up, I was still in the games.

I ran up the street to the parlor, and took the elevator to the only refuge there was for me. Kyra would be happy to relieve me and reprieve me. I'd bury my head in her furry pussy and hide there.

I stepped out of the elevator into a crying shame. My dearly beloved place of business had been trashed. Justine was not at her desk—her desk had been hacked apart with an ax. I looked up and down the corridor of cubicles. Doors had been busted in, towels thrown everywhere. Black paint had been splotched on the cream-colored walls. I walked from cubicle to cubicle, looking at the damage. None of them were occupied. It was like an evil whirlwind had blown through the parlor and sucked the girls out their windows.

My first guess was that it had been the Russians doing some drastic downsizing, but then I noticed the cross.

Someone had painted a big, black cross on the wall behind Justine's desk. There were words written above it:

"BUT EACH ONE IS TEMPTED WHEN HE IS CARRIED AWAY AND ENTICED IN HIS OWN LUST. THEN WHEN LUST HAS CONCEIVED, IT GIVES BIRTH TO SIN, AND WHEN SIN IS ACCOMPLISHED, IT BRINGS FORTH DEATH."

"Death" was underlined, so the reader would get the message fast.

It was still wet. The black paint came away on my fingertips. As I stood there, it was like I had an out-of-body experience. I was shaking and looking around for something to rub out that big black bastard of a cross, and at the same time I was high in the air looking down on a mob of people carrying crosses: fanatics, fundamentalists, holy rollers, snake handlers, people who would not only cast the first stone, but a bomb too. It seemed like I'd been running from them all my life—television hypocrites like Robin's father and his goons. Mr. Hopper, in particular.

They filled the courtroom in my head, yelling for my blood. Live your life against their rules, and they'll crucify you if they can. Hang you up on a cross and torture you, just like they did sweet Jesus.

Death was what their religion was about. I felt like puking.

"Buddy? Is that you, Buddy?" It was Kyra, who'd come up on the elevator. She looked scared, but they hadn't hurt her. Seeing her brought me back to reality, or within speaking distance of it.

"What the hell happened? Are you okay?"

She nodded. "They wanted you, Buddy."

"*Who* wanted me?"

"It was that street preacher. You know, the one I told you pays two bills for a blow job?"

I remembered him from the street corner where he'd cursed us through his microphone. The hypocrite and his gang of crows. They had come through with a fire ax and paint cans and tore the place apart. When Justine called the cops on them, they painted the sign of the cross and left. Naturally, when the cops came, they busted Justine and all the girls but Kyra. Hauled their asses off.

She looked embarassed for the first time since I'd known her. "I got a friend on the cops. A girl's got to look out for herself."

"The Russians are not going to be happy about this."

"They're mad. They saw me on the street after they found out. I told them it was the preacher."

Every cloud has a silver lining. Maybe, I thought, Kyra's survival instincts should be studied. There was a lot I could probably learn from her.

"What are you going to do, Buddy? What's going on?"

I owed her an explanation, but it was just too complicated to sort out for her right then.

"Well, I guess we're out of a job."

"Oh, the Russians will put it back together. They'll go bail. Give it a week, the parlor will be open again."

We took the elevator down, and stepped cautiously out on the street. It was gray and damp, like it always was in New York, but winter was almost over. I felt like my insides had been sucked out of me. I knew I could have gone home to Queens with Kyra, and I probably should have done that. We got along.

But I couldn't talk to her about what was in my head—about Christians, and courtrooms, and Robin and Ollie. Everything was mixed up, and she wouldn't understand. So I put her on the train to Queens and promised I'd see her next week.

Then I went to a pay phone and called Kat, to tell her I was coming.

29

A man with a load of grief knocked heavily on her door. She took one look at him and went to get the vodka. There was a need in his eyes that she hadn't seen before. He took the bottle from her, accepted a glass, poured and drank.

"What's happened? You look like hell." The words came out sounding harsher than she intended. He looked like he'd lost definition—he was blurry, and his fingertips were black.

"That's better than how I feel," he conceded.

She waited for him to explain while he drank another glass and then collapsed, a loose bundle of wires and rods, into her Morris chair.

"I don't know. . . ." he began.

Then he shook his head, as if struggling against the need to speak.

"I'm tired."

This is the turning point, she thought. Despite herself, she was resentful that she knew so much about him, already. She stiffened inwardly against being pulled into his need.

"Maybe you shouldn't talk."

Thinking, maybe something can be saved of our bargain, if only I don't learn anything more about who he is. If only he will spare me his secrets.

He stared at the crucifixes on her wall, and she wished she had taken them down. All they'd brought her was trouble. But although she understood now why he reacted so violently to them, it was her nature to challenge, not to ameliorate.

"They make me crazy," he told her, pointing a black finger at them accusingly. He told her what happened at the massage parlor. "They're after me, Kat."

"I know that, Buddy," she replied softly, almost sorrowfully. She resisted sympathy, deliberately hardening her heart against him.

He stared at her, as if, hearing his name, he failed to recognise the syllables. She watched as the realization sank in—that because she knew about him, their game was ending.

"Robin?"

She shook her head. "Miranda. She's Miranda now."

"So you know? She told you about us?"

"More than I ever wanted to hear."

"Well, that tears it," he sighed. "Don't it?"

"Yes."

There was an edge in her voice, icy and sharp, that bordered on barely concealed contempt. She remembered how powerful he'd seemed at the Club Subterranean, and the scenes that had followed, intense and darkly thrilling. How they had opened her up and forced her to grow. Then what flashed into her mind was a new image of him with an apron on, doing dishes.

She stood over him, erect, head thrown back, eyes stern. It was the way she had looked the first moment he saw her.

"The picture keeps changing. I can't keep up."

132

She frowned. "Don't feel sorry for yourself—that isn't allowed in my presence. Don't worry, I'll take care of you."

But he couldn't stop himself, he wept.

30

K yra was right. Justine reopened the Paradise Massage Parlor three days after the cross painting. In order to cover the black splotches, she'd had the place paneled, so that it reminded me of a trailer whorehouse in Nevada. There were fresh flowers in each cubicle. Back behind her command center—a new black metal desk—she stuck her considerable chest out to welcome what customers the creaky elevator coughed up. Business was off, of course—word gets around fast—but it cheered me up to hear that the Russians had mopped the street with the preacher and his deacons. Don't get between a Russian and his investment.

Being back at work helped put things in perspective. I did some thinking about Robin and Kat and decided that I'd let myself get too tangled in their webs. It was always a mistake to trust women you felt anything for, I told myself. So I took Star's advice, and put Kat out of my mind. If we got back together, things would be upside down, and I was off balance anyway. Robin was harder to push away, because I kept thinking of how she'd whipped Ollie. When I thought of that, I thought of her with her father. How surprised he'd looked—and sick-happy—that day.

Being Buddy Tate is not easy, but I try not to give myself much sympathy. As long as I could get it up, I'd get by.

At the parlor, I could distract myself with the pros. Pay them or not, they give good value without making you crazy. Kyra and I were best the fuck buddies, but I liked the Spanish girl, Benita, too. She was a change from Kyra's flat chestedness. Benita's boobs were oversized balloons on her tiny brown frame, but they were real, and capped with black nipples like raisins. She told me she was mostly Indian, and she knew secrets. When Kyra was busy with a customer and too much peeping had made me goatish, I would often go ask Benita if she would do me a favor.

What she would do when she saw the painful condition I was in, was get her hands oily and rub them up and down the big boy, pinching and squeezing and looking cute as she did it. Then she would lie down on a mattress we placed on the floor, I would straddle her, and we would do a titty fuck. While she pressed those balloons around it, I would slide in and out of the crevice she created. By bending her neck, she could just reach the tip of my dick with her tongue. We usually got a good rhythm going this way, and then she would want me to put it in her. Even after I went down on her, she was so tight it was like copping her cherry every time she spread for me. But she would slowly suck me up into her belly and then—this was one of her tricks— hold me there. No matter how hard I tried to pull out of her, she could hold me with her muscles. Indian.

Meanwhile, she'd whisper to me, "You like my *cho-cha*, Buddy? I keep it hot for you. You *like* it?"

I liked it, and I showed it. We got so hot together we

sizzled. She never took her black eyes off my face, so she could see reflected every twinge, spasm and crackle of my pleasure. And all the while we were face to face, I was sucking on her nipples, squeezing those big flesh bulbs and wishing they were milk fountains. I had a fantasy of those dark nipples spraying me all over, so that I was dripping with her sweet cream.

Between getting that kind of action at the massage parlor, and tearing off a piece with Cyd the submissive when Star was busy working on a client, I was feeling like my old self again, ready for raunch. What else did I need? Certainly not spider women.

Women like Kyra and Benita didn't play games. They put out for pay and mostly enjoyed their work. They knew what I wanted and they were happy to give it. When I unzipped, they knew exactly how I felt about them. It was a good arrangement.

But nothing is as simple as it looks at first, not with women. I was seeing a lot of Benita, and one night after I'd just hosed her down—coming in her *chocha* and then pulling out to slip it between her titties—she wiped herself off and gave me a serious look.

"No more, Buddy. I can't do you no more like this."

I was puzzled. I thought at first she was thinking about her family in San Salvador, and that maybe I should be paying her. But that wasn't it. It was a matter of the heart, she said. Kyra was like a sister to her. When I said I didn't see what that had to do with anything, she let me know I'd said the wrong thing.

"*Ay*, Buddy. You're a coyote. You think it's all just fucking."

"Well?"

"Kyra is a nice girl."

"A very nice girl," I agreed, thinking of her black bush, and how eager she was when we did it. But Benita gave me a sentimental, pained look and I knew I was in trouble again.

"You stupid, *hombre*? She loves you."

Oh, shit. There was that word that didn't mean anything, because it could mean whatever anybody wanted it to mean. People loved their cars, loved their pets, loved their money, loved their coffee, loved their mothers, loved their football teams, loved their jobs, loved their country, loved their television programs—there was no end of loving. So when someone said it, it meant nothing to me. Hate had a shape. It was tangible.

How could Kyra love me? She didn't know me. But Benita wouldn't listen. She was cutting off the *chocha* supply. No more titty fucks and fantasies of fountains of cream.

So I went to see Kyra. When I saw her face, I could tell the two of them had planned what they intended to happen.

"I thought you knew how I feel about you, Buddy," she said.

I could have objected that I didn't know—and didn't want to know—all night. It wouldn't have made a difference.

Still, I tried. "You know who I am, Kyra? You get the best part of me everytime we do it. All I am is my dick. Love's barking up the wrong tree. *Love*'s just a word, like *fuck*. I like *fuck* better."

She gave me a pitying look, like she knew I didn't mean what I was saying—like I was just playing tough guy.

"I'll do anything for you, Buddy. I'll be your slut, I'll be your whore. I'll turn tricks a hundred times a day and give all the money to you." I could see that she meant it.

"You're crazy. We've got a nice thing going here, Kyra. We both enjoy it. Why mess it up?"

Reason wasn't Kyra's strong point. She took my hand and placed it on her chest between her breasts and held it there. Her heart was racing like a little bird trying to escape her chest, beating its wings faster and faster.

It was her willingness that was beating there, and it made me feel like a bastard because I wanted to reach into her chest and crush it. She was giving herself to me just as Robin had at first, and Kat. But she was announcing the price with every beat of her heart. Kyra with the come-filled eyes was mine—if I would be hers. I was kidding myself to think that I could have a strictly sexual relationship with any woman.

31

Kat played with Robin in the hours she could steal from work—and Olivier's imperious demands for assistance in the promotion of his book. While cuddled together in Kat's huge throne bathtub they spoke of Buddy. They giggled and whispered secrets about what they might do with him. But weeks passed, and he didn't appear as they expected.

By mid-April she was sure she missed him when, one morning after another sleepless night, she rose and took down her crucifixes, wrapping them carefully and putting them in the back of her closet. At work she called for an appointment with Buddy's friend, Star. She would have herself tattooed, it was long overdue.

That evening she took a taxi to Star's smudged old building on Houston Street. She pressed a button under a brass plate that said ASTERION STUDIOS, was buzzed in, and walked up one flight to the door of his loft.

One of the most amazing creatures she'd ever seen opened the door. She was a small redhead wearing black lipstick, an iron collar, and nothing else. She had a tough face and a body illustrated with tattooing and a huge purple birthmark.

"Are you Kat?"

"Yes." It was true; Katherine was no more.

"He said you were tall."

Kat followed her into a large black cave, illuminated by stalagmitic candles on a table. She saw two leather couches and a coffee table at one end, and a bull-like man rising to greet her. It was very warm in the room, and he was bare chested. His smell was strong but not objectionable. A tattooed dragon rose between his nipples, each of which sported multiple piercings. As she came closer to him, she saw the star between his shaggy eyebrows winking at her. His was a powerful presence, reminding her of photographs of Picasso bare chested.

"Buddy said you were tall," he rumbled.

She looked around, but the ranks of sputtering candles that flickered everywhere revealed no lurking Buddy, waiting to surprise her. They did, however, show her a large steel cage in one corner.

"I think he probably said more than that about me," she smiled, projecting as much confidence as she could muster.

"He said that you didn't have any tattoos, anywhere."

"Is he here, by any chance?"

"Look, when you called, you said you wanted a tattoo. I'd heard about you, so I said okay. But I'm not a matchmaker. I put ink on skin, and my time is valuable."

His brusqueness was dismissive, and Kat felt her confidence faltering. She swallowed.

"I'm here for a tattoo."

"What kind?" His large dark eyes were skeptical.

"A blue butterfly."

"A butterfly?" he said sarcastically. "A *blue* butterfly, did you say?" He snorted with disdainful contempt, and shook his head.

"What's wrong with that?" she asked.

"I don't do tourist junk. You come here for an original, fine. Not butterflies. Not panthers, not scrolls that say 'Mom.' " She had insulted his artistry.

"But this is a special kind of butterfly. It would take an artist to do one the way I want it done." She reached into her bag for a news photo, in color, of a blue morpho. He held it at arm's length, his eyebrows scrunched up so the star positively twinkled with malefic force.

"So this is what everybody's been talking about."

He rubbed his chin as he considered it. "Lot of detailing." Something told her that he was playing with her.

"Buddy told you about it?"

"He mentioned it."

"What do you think?"

"It'll cost you." He named a price that made her wince, but she nodded.

"It'll be my own interpretation. . . ."

"Of course."

He gave her an appraising look, but this time she saw that he was wondering where she wanted her first tattoo.

"Where do you want it?"

"Someplace where only my lover can see it."

"Tit?"

She shook her head.

"Butt?"

She nodded.

Later in the evening, Star opened up. He talked nonstop, in fact, while he bent over her ass with his needle. His deep voice exercised a hypnotic effect on her. She was also being aroused more than she had anticipated.

His touch on her bare skin was professional, but she hadn't expected to enjoy the bite of the needle so much. Her insides were liquefying, and soon he would be able to smell her. This was a ceremony as intimate as intercourse, she realized. He is penetrating me, leaving a permanent impression. She wondered if he was having a sexual reaction, squeezing and pinching her buttock.

She asked him about Miranda's tattooing, and he told her that he had created a design to cover her scars. He resisted her questions about Buddy, but then told her how he saw his friend.

"Buddy's on his own plane—you might even say he's in his own dimension. I wouldn't know how to explain him to anyone. You just have to look at him as a kind of mutation. Or maybe somebody dropped from another planet."

"What do you mean?"

"Buddy's not crazy. He's not bad. Hell, he's not even a pervert. It's just that using that donkey dick of his is his purpose in life. I mean, who knows? Maybe the Greeks and Romans were right about there being many gods who come to earth as people. You ever hear of Priapus? You know, the god with the big . . . ? Well, that's Buddy Tate."

They took a break. He gave her a chenille robe to put on, handed her a Dos Equis he produced from a small refrigerator, and led her into the candlelit main room, flexing his fingers as he continued his monologue.

"Buddy takes women too seriously. That's what I always tell him. He thinks he's just after sex, and he gets involved anyway. He can't help himself."

She asked if he knew about their arrangement.

"Yeah, yeah. You tell him stories about fucking other people, he promises not to tell you anything about himself. It's like the kind of deal people make all the time.

Look at Cyd and me, for example. But deals always run out. . . ."

The redhead had crept in to sit at Star's feet, crouched like a faithful dog, her slightly crossed eyes impassive. Her illustrated body gleamed in the candlelight.

"Cyd comes to me and says she'll be my slave. All I have do is fill every inch of her skin with ink. We have a deal. That's life—especially between boys and girls. You know what I mean?"

"I was afraid if I learned anything about him, I'd be disappointed."

"So you made a real person into a figment of your imagination. That's hard to get away with."

"I wanted him to take me into the world he knew— and I didn't. I wanted him to teach me."

Star shook his head disgustedly at this, and placed his bottle on the coffee table. Cyd opened another for him. "Chicks. You all want things your way, or you won't play. Buddy's no match for you, or Robin."

Kat shifted on the couch to take the pressure off her newly tattooed buttock. She was feeling somewhat overwhelmed by Star's opinions, and Star's needles. With her ability to detach herself from any situation and see it as from above—as if she were simply bodiless intelligence—she saw the bizarreness of the scene she was in. She was sitting in a cave, listening to a man with a star between his eyebrows tell her about the man she'd loved—maybe. And she couldn't deny the effect of his personality, and the intimacy they'd shared as the blue morpho was etched into her buttock. She was turned on, and she didn't know what to do about it. Cyd seemed to be glowering at her, as if protecting her master from such a willful, selfish woman.

Then she decided what she wanted, and she stopped thinking of the other woman as a barrier to Star. Once she made up her mind, things always seemed to flow. In her detachment, she saw Cyd as an avenue to learning something that she had to learn. Something that had been in the back of her mind since she'd arrived.

The cage. She turned her head to look at it, as if measuring it for her body. It was the thing in the room that frightened her most, and it was her nature to go straight to what frightened her.

"Who gets to use the cage?" she asked. She hoped she didn't sound coy.

He didn't miss a beat when he said, "Oh, that's reserved for very bad girls."

"How bad?" It was a request, not a question, that she posed.

"Girls like you," he responded. He exchanged a glance with Cyd that was telepathic in its scope—and gleeful, she thought.

"I want to," she said, standing up.

Cyd rose and came to help her remove her robe. Her decision made, Kat stood naked before them, ready to take the next step down. Why waste time?

Then she was crawling on all fours backwards into the cage, its metal floor cold against her knees, and the door was locked. The key made a snicking sound that was very final, she thought, and then she tried to put all thoughts out of her mind, feeling claustrophobic pressures on every side. She was forced to crouch on all fours like an animal, while her vision was limited to her captors' legs. The legs moved around her, and then Cyd's face leered through the bars at her, asking:

"Sure you're ready for this, baby?" She chuckled raspily.

Kat growled back at her, the sound coming out involuntarily, and she took a deep breath, surrendering herself to her reptile brain—the brain that told her that she was an animal, with claws and teeth, and with a need for her body to be caged, so that what was caged still inside might fly free from her throat.

Her punishment forced her to calm herself. Divorced from her body, she could see with absolute detachment that she had done the right thing.

For they both excited her. She felt his hand on her ass again, and rested her cheek on her hands against the steel cage floor, arching her back so that she could move her butt with infinitely satisfying slowness. The redhead's slutty vulpine face made a frank promise to hold nothing back.

She was dry, and found herself sucking on her fingers. Water was flicked into her face, and when she looked there was a bottle like those attached to hamster cages, a black nipple curving from it. She adjusted her long body so that she could suck at it, lapping the water she sucked out. She was a baby, she took what she needed, and then she wet herself.

When they opened the door of the cage, it took her a moment to recognize her freedom, and gather her forces to crawl out to it. She rested on the floor, looking at their boots. They were talking, and then she was pulled to her knees and forced back. A metal collar was snapped around her neck—it was snug, but not constricting—and a padlock attached to a chain held her, as if on a leash. Her wrists and forearms were wrapped tightly together by coiled rope.

She welcomed this further punishment as she had welcomed certain ceremonial occasions in church. The prescribed postures in each aided in achieving the right meditative acceptance of suffering.

She gasped when Cyd began pulling her nipples, twisting and pinching them, then cupping her fire-tipped breasts and squeezing them, with painful pressure. When she thought she might black out, the pressure lessened for an instant, and then she felt clothespins being attached to her outraged, tender nipples.

After enduring this, she was pulled to her feet and pushed in the direction of the couch, and then down to her knees again. She faced Star in a subservient, captive position.

But she didn't feel inferior, in any way. She was on fire, she was clear as glass, and she was filled with gratitude—directed not at him or Cyd, but for having been shown what she possessed when all else was taken away. This cruel, welcome freedom.

She was happy when he stood up and unzipped, pulling out his flaccid dark penis. He moved close to her and she could smell him. If this was to be her reward, it was one she hadn't dared hope for. But he wanted her hair. He stood over her and held up her long auburn hair, wrapping it around his penis like coils of silk. Then he stopped, and moved to stand at the end of the couch. Kat watched disappointedly as Cyd moved into what was obviously a familiar position. She wriggled her body so that her head inclined over the arm of the couch, under Star's limp penis. While Cyd adjusted herself, Kat looked at the woman's firm body, and noticed a tattoo of a blue butterfly.

Star's scorn came back to her. Now she felt she didn't know anything.

"Buddy said you couldn't give him a good blow job."

"I tried, but you know, he's just. . . ."

"Watch this." Cyd swallowed his limpness.

32

When I walked in, it was after midnight. The candles were going out, but I could see Cyd on the couch, giving Star some super head, and a woman wrapped up tight as a bug in a rug, watching them. Some new toy they were showing off to, I thought.

I felt like Kyra had sucked out my blood and liquefied my bones, and I was getting old quick. Working at the Paradise Massage Parlor was taking its toll. Women drove a hard bargain.

When you leave yourself open the way I had, you get fed on. When you let yourself feel something, they can grab at you. Robin still had a good grip on my nuts, no matter how I tried to tell myself different. (I couldn't call her by her new name, Miranda; she wasn't that— she wasn't his.) Now that I knew where she was, it was hard staying away from her—but if I didn't, I knew I could kiss my stones goodbye. Either way, I was squeezed.

I watched Cyd do Star as I had so many times, and felt myself being brought back to life. Cyd gives everything she's got to the task at hand, I'll tell you. I knew how good her tongue would feel. I felt like a moth being drawn to a light, heading for them.

I almost stumbled over the woman kneeling on the floor, who was also watching. I looked closer. It was Kat, looking up at me.

"Buddy?" It sounded sweet and helpless, the way she said my name. I saw the clothespins sticking out from her big nipples, and knew how turned on she was, so I leaned down and twisted one of the clothespines. She gasped.

"I was somebody else the last time you saw me," I admitted to her.

I was feeling much worse, then. I thought I could handle her this time around. "That's not who I am."

"You can be that, too, Buddy. I've missed you."

I looked over at the scene on the couch before I got down on the floor next to her. Star looked me straight in the eye, and I could see he was about to let loose. Cyd had swallowed him, balls and all.

"What's she doing here?" I called to him.

"Ah, don't be too hard on her, Buddy. She had an exceptionally educational experience this evening." He laughed that crazy devil's laugh of his.

Kat looked different, I had to notice that. She was looser. There was a new spark in her eye. It was like someone had turned a pilot light on inside her. She had heated up, and it made her prettier.

"You know anything new?" I asked her, twisting a clothespin again. "Did you learn anything from these two?"

She showed me those even white teeth I liked to run my tongue over. I didn't know if she was smiling, or ready to spit, but I knew I wanted this new Kat. Maybe, after all, she was the one who could make me forget

Robin. Or maybe, the flesh is always weak when it's confronted with a tied up, naked woman.

It didn't take her long to answer my question about what she'd learned. "Let me show you."

That's how easy it was for her to pull me back into her web.

33

Eulalie was worried about Olivier. She wondered if he was not coming apart. His face was puffy, and there were dark circles under his eyes. Ever since they'd come to New York and he'd married that broken doll, Miranda, he had especially worried her. She had always taken care of him, and she continued heroically in this thankless role, but at the price of feeling perpetually tense. She could not afford to snap. He needed her.

My Life as a Monster was well launched. Reviewers had been properly respectful of his behind-the-scenes stories of fabulous financial coups, but less receptive to his erotic confessions and theories. Television interviewers had asked the inevitable questions about liaisons with actresses and models, but were made nervous by his urgent need to talk about sex. He grew increasingly frustrated as he saw how America wanted to compartmentalize him. American journalists took sexuality seriously only when it was particularized and scandalous. Ideas were anathema.

He directed the campaign for his book from his hotel bed—constantly on the phone with Katherine, speaking to powerful media people, arguing with Miranda, directing his myriad business interests. Eulalie was kept busy running errands, directing the mundane affairs of his life, and worrying.

She liked it best—on those rare occasions when he had no engagements—when she had him to herself. Together, they could pursue the little eccentric moments that they both loved.

Sometimes he would talk to her for hours, while she simply and happily tended to him. As she listened, she would shave his body, massage it, oil it and even squeeze the blackheads on his broad back. It was like taking care of herself, a symbiotic relationship that erased the boundaries between their bodies. If he had a cough, her lungs contracted; if he sneezed, she did also.

She scolded him, too, as she might scold herself.

She had finished manicuring his nails, and walked into the bathroom, leaving the door open so that he could hear her from the bed. They spoke in French, as they always did.

"It's not right that you make a fool of yourself, just to sell a book. You are throwing yourself away. . . ."

He blocked out her words—complaints he knew by heart—and listened for what came next. He suspected that she guessed how he responded to hearing the splash of her water in the toilet, but he had never told her. Bold as he was about his most catholic tastes, some he kept to himself as being too subtle for others to appreciate.

The sound of Eulalie tinkling was one of those small quotidian pleasures he thought he could never explain, but it tickled his aural imagination. He had no desire to watch her in the act of urination—not up close, at least—but the sound thrilled him. He savored it now as she flushed, and continued her harangue. When she reentered the room, he pretended to listen to her warnings, but he was really thinking about the stiffening she had unknowingly caused. She knew him well, but he had spied on her secretly. Now, would she notice the effect she'd had, and wonder why, out of nowhere—?

"I don't think you are listening to me, Olivier. I think your health is being affected, as well as your dignity. . . ."

He tuned her out again, smiling to himself at the solidity of his erection under the covers. Here was yet another gift from the gods he worshipped. There must be something new they could do, to enjoy this gift.

If only his wife would walk into the room at this moment, he would make them fight over it—and maybe out of the conflict would be born a new, as yet unnamed, pleasure. In his book he heaped contumely on the twentieth century's sexologists, even the great Wilhelm Reich. Olivier's mind was so stocked with obscure perversions, so open to erotic nuance, so sensitive to the slightest stirring of lust, that he had proclaimed himself in his book the sexual prophet of the new century. But it was his imagination, he was certain, that continued to provide him with erections.

"I will make them acknowledge who I am in the sexual realm. Then I will be happy, Eulalie. For most people, life is an either or proposition. If this, then not that. A simple, Hegelian view of the processes of life. I want to show them that there is another way to regard sex. Like every philosopher, I want to offer my prescription to heal the insanity of the world."

But she knew this. These words were from a prepared speech he made whenever they would give him more than the opportunity for a sound bite.

"You are becoming a crusader. It doesn't sit well with you."

"Americans like crusaders," he retorted.

"Not those with positive words about such intimate

matters," she shot back. "Not a European who can write in his book about The Maze."

Indeed, his concept of The Maze had drawn the most criticism from reviewers. Most of them couldn't believe that an internationally known financial figure would confess to creating such a game to amuse himself. He offered it as a demonstration, to back up his theories about the evolution of polymorphous perversity, but they took it as evidence of his insensitivity to matters of gender and class.

He didn't wish to argue with Eulalie. He would lose his opportunity. He decided that he had to take action. He considered each of the direct ways she might bring him to orgasm.

He made use of her mouth almost every day. She was avid and expert at bringing him to climax orally, especially inspired at biting with just enough pressure. Her cunt was her best erotic feature, because she could spurt her juices after he had penetrated her deeply enough, for a sufficient length of time. Her ass was problematic, for she was sometimes cursed with hemorrhoids. He liked to catch her bending over a sink, or a table, lift her skirt from behind, and take her quickly. She had trained her body to respond to his needs with dispatch, but he was sometimes impatiently rough.

Often, when they were watching television together, he would have her take it out and play with it—doing a little light paddling of his penis—almost as occupational therapy. She liked to knit, and didn't mind keeping her fingers busy as they watched a news program or the occasional pornographic video. Constant stimulation kept him in tune.

But these were standard pleasures.

He couldn't decide. He grasped himself under the covers and squeezed hard, to keep it firm.

She was still talking, trying to convince him that it was time to return to France. Spring in the chateau at Cagnes-sur-mer, or on the yacht at Saint-Tropez. They would lie in the sun, and the dark circles would disappear from under his eyes. Perhaps she would spend time with her sister. . . .

Then she was flapping the air about her head excitedly, crying out that there was a bee in the room. It must have come in with the flowers, or down from the roof gardens five stories above them. She chased it with a rolled-up newspaper as it hummed slowly around the room, looking for an exit.

To the man who is receptive to accident, blessed with a rich imagination, the gods deliver what is sought.

"No! Don't kill it, Eulalie! I must have it—catch it somehow, and bring it to me."

The urgency in his voice alerted her. She turned to see that he had thrown off the covers to show her what his inspiration was. She understood at once, and set about catching the hapless bee in an expertly wielded towel. It was a matter of moments before she transferred the stunned Erinys to a fluted champagne glass.

He confined it with his palm and watched it staggering, unable to fly, or climb the glass. This harbinger of spring had been sent to him expressly for his purposes.

Shaking the glass to arouse the bee's anger was the only preparation he needed. As Eulalie watched with open mouth and glazed eyes, he plunged his penis into the glass at the insect.

34

After an intimate dinner by candlelight, Kat and Miranda climbed into a hot bath with a bottle of Remy Martin, and turned their attention to the small portable television on Katherine's vanity. They left Buddy at the kitchen sink doing the dishes.

They were set to watch a popular cable interview show that claimed to reach the most adventurous minds in America. This booking had been Katherine's biggest coup in directing the publicity campaign for Olivier's bestselling—and increasingly controversial—memoir.

The program titles came on, and then a shot filled the small screen of Olivier de Carlo, looking arrogantly distinguished in his tailored blue windowpane-checked suit and black silk scarf. Opposite him sat a fussy little man with the face of a Pomeranian.

The host's first question to Olivier was about the shaky world economy, and then followed a series of financial questions which Olivier answered with evident, mounting impatience. There was a station break. When the program continued, the interviewer sneered as he ventured a question about the scandalous sexual revelations and opinions in *My Life as a Monster*. Olivier seized his opportunity.

"I have nothing to say about reproductive sex. That is about plumbing, and production quotas. What I talk about in my book is the effect the erotic has had on my life. I have grown into a man who savors all the exquisite sexual perversities—I use this ignorant term only so I will be understood—because my erotic nature was highly developed at an early age. It came to me like a gift—a receptivity to all the erotic possibilities. Without this gift, I doubt that I could have kept my sanity. . . ."

"Yes, yes," the interviewer interrupted, not understanding a thing. "But what does this have to do with your business acumen—your startling successes in the market?"

"Being open to eros freed me to be open to everything else. It freed me to see the world with fresh eyes—to see opportunities everywhere. You see, various powers rule us—political, psychological, biological—and keep us blindfolded to what is truly possible. I am a man who lives his life without a blindfold."

"So, you mean to say that if we paid more attention to our sex lives, we'd do better in the market?" The Pomeranian chuckled derisively.

"That is the kind of stupid question I was afraid you might ask," Olivier replied haughtily.

"He's going to lose it now," Miranda predicted, spilling some of her brandy into the bath water as she sat up straight. But Kat's mind had strayed to Buddy. They had cinched him into a corset, tightened a dog collar around his neck, and stuffed his muscular legs into stockings. A ball gag in his mouth prevented unwanted speech. He had come back to her, and this costume was both his punishment and reward.

When Kat focused back on the television screen, Olivier was holding up *My Life as a Monster* and leafing through it. He had asked to read a passage, in response to a hostile question about how he had discovered his erotic proclivities. He was smiling to himself.

As soon as he began to read, Kat recognized disaster. "Oh, my God," she said softly, carefully setting her glass down on a table next to the tub. Miranda, who had never bothered to read her husband's book, listened with growing revulsion on her features.

"When I was little," Olivier began, as if reading a fairy tale, "I liked to crunch bugs. Those hard-shelled large beetles that were common where I grew up near Aix. I would catch them in a glass milk bottle—dozens of them—and then take them into our family's big tile-floored kitchen, where I would release them. At first, I stepped on them with my shoes, but later I danced on them with my bare feet. The combination of killing, with the pain their horny carapaces caused against my tender soles, provided me with an exquisite, sensuous thrill. . . ."

Olivier looked up from his book, smiling broadly at the camera. The screen went black for a minute, and then they were watching a public service message about safety belts.

"*Ugh!*" Miranda exclaimed. "He's insane—I told you so. Buddy and I should have dropped him off the balcony."

They had planned some serious body play for Buddy. The telecast set the tone for the evening that followed.

35

They wrapped Buddy in a cocoon of bright chains, strapped his wrists to the spindle headboard of Kat's bed, and stood naked over him. He was in their possession. Nothing was planned, but they would see if he was trainable. Spontaneous evenings. . . .

The ball gag in his mouth ensured his silence, but his solemnly watchful eyes told them they had his full attention. They had left his penis exposed, and it lay limp on the chains along his inner thigh, a sleeping serpent.

Kat brushed the tips of her breasts over Buddy's eyes so that he could admire her new piercings.

Then she whispered in his ear, "This is the last story, Buddy. I'm going to make it hot."

She looked down to see what effect her words might have had, and saw the snake awaken.

"Are you a good bottom, Buddy? We hope so, because it's the only way we can keep you now, and we're very . . . attached to you."

Miranda stood over him as she did in his dreams, a whip coiled in her hand. She wore heels because Kat liked to watch her ass move. She looked very angry with him. He drew back from her, but she pressed close and spat in his face. She had fangs.

"You shouldn't have followed me, Buddy. You know how bad I am." Spitting this, hissing.

He could expect the worst. He smiled.

That was enough for awhile. They would savor their possession of him and talk like devil sisters about what he meant to them.

"We should put blinders and a ball gag on his penis, since that's what he thinks with," Kat giggled, watching as it slowly filled with blood.

"I know he can take a lot of suffering. I guess when you choose Buddy's path you'd better be able to!" Cold laughter.

"He said he owned me. I believed him."

"He said he wanted me to be his mirror." Oh, they were sisters.

Lying there, listening to them, Buddy couldn't stop his own thoughts from wandering. He was in the zone—tensely expectant and alive, yet curiously relaxed, almost indifferent. Things would happen in their own time, and Kat would tell him the story as it unfolded.

I've been here before, he thought. Women standing over me with whips. Women with fangs in bloody mouths. Naked women strongly in control. Sisters in charge. Images rolled through his mind:

Again and again, like I never get tired of it. Over and over, like I never want to roll the big boy up and put a combination lock on my zipper. In and out, like I'll never learn. Same-old same-old habits. Take off one mask and there's another. Pull that one off and rip off your face. Put on a costume, take off a costume. Do it, and *do it again and again*.

And every time it's new, and every time, you find a

little more of what you're looking for. So of course you do it again.

Sensing that Buddy's focus had shifted from them, Miranda started work on his feet. She put down her whip and picked up a thick magazine with which she slapped the soles of his feet. When he jerked them away, she followed. He could not resist because his knees were wrapped in the cocoon of chains.

"He doesn't like his feet tickled," Miranda complained at last, with tired forearms.

"I don't know about that," Kat said, indicating Buddy's tell-tale erection. "But why don't we see if he prefers to have his ass whipped?" She was an avid student.

They freed him of his chains, and then reattached his restraints, drawing him closer to the headboard so that he was bent over pillows with his muscular buttocks in the air.

Four hands squeezed and pinched at his flesh, then four hands rained slaps on it, harder and harder. His erection strained against the firm mattress. The slaps became smacks, and then they used a paddle.

I can take this, Buddy thought. Pain's just a head trip. He was beginning to warm up, but he wasn't anywhere near full throttle yet. There's no game I can't play when I'm turned on to it.

He heard laughter and turned his face on the bed, straining to look up. The strap-on Kat wore was almost as big as the boss. She was greasing it up, and looking at him like he had looked at her the first time he fucked her. Serious desire.

She was his mirror . . . Their lusts were interchangeable. She had learned everything he taught her.

When she mounted him and forced the tip of the dildo into his anus, she used words he might have used, the dirty words made clean in the act: "I am going to fuck you, Buddy. I'm going to put my big prick right up there and make you whimper. I'm going to fuck this tight little cunt you've got. I'm going to see if you have any limits with a dick up you."

In and out, in and out. Push pull, push pull. Again and again.

She took her time and fucked him hard, but he didn't think her heart was in it. He guessed she was putting on a show for Miranda, that what was happening in the room was all about what was between them. He was property, at this moment, and nothing more. And he was soft, pressed against the mattress.

They took a break, and brewed tea. They were pacing themselves. He had no idea how far they would take this, but he didn't think Miranda was ready to call it an evening. He could count on her to push it, he was sure of that.

"I like your teeth," he heard Kat say to Miranda. "Are they real?"

Miranda's response was inaudible. He thought of her small, even, sparkling teeth. He knew they were more dangerously real than any fangs; he'd seen them stained with her father's blood.

"I like your tattoo," Miranda replied politely. They moved away from the bed and continued talking, but he couldn't understand them. Someone flushed the toilet. He remembered their scene with her husband on the balcony, and wondered if he'd felt nervous, listening. Wondered if, like him, he wanted Miranda for things like this.

Then they were back. His anticipation rose.

"Do you like Kat's tattoo, Buddy?"

He remembered the blue butterfly on her butt. He remembered, too, the butterfly exhibit where he'd gone to meet her. The cold splash on his sore buttock told him what they were going to do next.

"We're going to brand you, Buddy."

Miranda put her head next to his on the bed again, and showed him the knife. She stuck out her tongue and licked the sharp tip. The look in her eyes was like bats flitting out of a cave, and he could tell that she was gone, that this time she might not be able to stop, that maybe Kat couldn't stop her—or wouldn't want to.

He was afraid for the first time with a fear that underlies every act in the game: that the actor may disappear into her role. He watched with helpless dread as she flicked a lighter and sterilized the point until it glowed.

The whip was not to fall. That would have been welcome next to the pain that accompanied the first cut. The subsequent incisions felt like screeching chalk over the blackboard of nerves in his lower back. They had reinforced his restraints so he could not writhe about; he was afraid to move, anyway. He bit down hard on the ball gag, Kat whispered in his ear:

"How do you like the story so far, Buddy?"

When they finished, they had cut a small butterfly into him. The cuts filled with blood, and they bent over him to lap like sisters at his brand, their foreheads almost touching.

After awhile they released him from his restraints, and gave him water to drink. They bandaged his buttock, and washed their mouths. He went to the bathroom to urinate. They had to help him, because his feet were so sore. As he stood there pissing, bent over like an old man, gingerly feeling his painful ass, he felt depleted: Finished. The big boy dangled uselessly, like a broken chain. But he'd told himself that if nothing else, a good top could also be a good bottom. You didn't have to be one or the other. Each was just a role, just the other side of the coin.

When he emerged, they were preparing for bed. Kat was brushing her teeth, walking around the room, humming to herself. Miranda was yawning. He shambled gratefully toward the bed, and them, envisioning himself sandwiched between their breasts. He brightened at the thought of what they might let him do with them in the morning. He had never had sisters before, not even self-adopted sisters.

But they had other plans. Taking him firmly by his arms, they pulled him to Kat's big shoe closet and shoved him into the dark, closing and locking the door. He lay there, sprawled across the racks and boxes of shoes, inhaling the rich leather smells, his face jammed into a pair of sandals. He raked them aside with one arm, trying to empty a narrow space in which to lie, and in so doing, knocked some heavy objects off a shelf. One banged into his forehead. Despite the paper it was wrapped in, his hands recognized the simple, deadly shape of a crucifix.

36

One warm Sunday afternoon in spring, Kat stalked into the American Museum of Natural History in her Doc Martens, wearing a heavy chain around her neck like an amulet, a skimpy tank top and a short leather skirt. Her long legs were bare and tanned. She had cut her hair short.

Men looked lingeringly and longingly at her smooth legs and her protuberant nipples. Women who dared looked into her eyes and melted when she boldly returned their stares.

She enjoyed her new power to attract, and had come to test it by picking up a partner for normal heterosexual intercourse, something simple and uncomplicated by roles and masks and costumes. She was in search of vanilla sex—the kind that had always satisfied her in the past, because she was beginning to worry that she'd stepped over some invisible line she wasn't meant to cross.

She continued to function well at work, although she was increasingly distracted by her new obsessions. Nothing else seemed to matter but the games, Buddy and

Miranda. Her past had fallen away from her. She was someone else.

She strode to the diorama that was her totem, and stood looking at the wolves. She was a hunter now, like them. Or was she? Was she, after playing so hard and seeing so much, still pretending? Was Kat a mask behind which Katherine waited, like a good little girl?

She hoped that a sexual encounter would serve as a reality check, that it might even shock her back into everyday paradigms of behavior. She was startled out of her reverie by a familiar voice. *We're always sent what we look for*, she thought.

"It's all wrong, you know," it rumbled, sounding knowledgable.

It was Garson the bear, whose heavy hand had sown the seed of her rebirth. She wondered if he even recognized her, or if his question was not asked dozens of times on this very spot every Sunday. She threw him a glance over her shoulder, and was gratified by the happy gleam of recognition in his eyes. The next minute he was embracing her in a bear hug which managed to charm and irritate her equally. She enjoyed feeling fragile, pressed to his tree trunk body, but she didn't like his male presumptiousness. His hands grazed her breasts.

"Katherine!"

She turned and smiled. He smacked his lips in hearty appreciation, looking over the costume of her transformation.

"Hello, Garson. You still like wolves, I see." She wet her lips.

"You're a new woman. Transformed, like a. . . ."

"A butterfly?" She rubbed the secret tattoo on her buttock.

He grinned broadly—inordinately sure of himself, she

thought. His eyes were fastened on her nipples as he spoke.

"Christ, I've had some wet dreams about you, Katherine. We had a memorable time together, didn't we?"

"I didn't have any complaints, Garson."

It was obvious that he had forgotten about the spanking he administered. Or perhaps it was part of his standard repertoire.

"Do you want to do it again?" He leered cheerfully at her. "Now?"

She nodded. "I was hoping you'd ask."

It was late afternoon, and long shadows were falling across Central Park West when they emerged from the museum. Garson surprised her by suggesting a walk in the park instead of hailing a taxi.

"I have a special spot I want to show you."

"I like beds, Garson. How much of a slut do you think I am?"

"You'll like this little bower, Katherine. It's out of the way of everything, and very private. It's like an Easter basket, really."

The park was red and green with spring. Skate boarders sailed past them, joggers split their ranks to go around them, and she followed him deeper into the park, no longer resisting this new adventure. After what she'd done in the dark, why not this?

They went through a tunnel, circled into the woods, bent under some bushes, and then crawled into what she had to agree was an Easter basket of soft grass and mosses, and colorful crocuses. Through the hedge she could see that they were not far from the zoo, where she loved watching the penguins in their tank, and the lascivious bonobo apes on their island outdoors.

"You're right, it's nice here," she said, opening her mouth to his probing tongue. His hand moved over her breasts, and pushed up under the tank top to fondle them; and then his bearded mouth was sucking hard at her nipples, his tongue flicking her new piercings.

She let him take the lead. She wanted to be able to monitor her responses to him. She knew he could make Katherine cry out in orgasm, but now Kat stood above their coupling, watching and weighing everything through a cruel lens that magnified every expected gesture, every inelegant grunt.

He had spread his tweed jacket for her to lie back on. He pushed up her skirt, as he had her top, and seemed visibly surprised that she wore no panties, and that she had shaved her vulva; but it also excited him, because he plunged his ursine head between her legs. She lay back, uncomfortable—but in comparison to what, she asked herself, a cage?—yet swept up in his passion, which was so much greater than what she felt.

Oh, she felt good. Garson was an expert, clearly, at tonguing and touching and squeezing and kissing. When he entered her, his enthusiasm could not be faulted, nor his energy. His thrusts were so hard and rapid that she felt like she was being driven into the ground by his immense drive to please her. She would be offered the gift of her orgasm in a gaily wrapped box, and she would rip it open with delight; it was foreordained. The man had a track record.

Knowing this, wanting this almost despite herself, Katherine forgot her discomfort, and reciprocated, finding the energy to thrust back up at him, to accept his penetration and increase its impact on the nerve endings in her vagina.

But Kat drew back fastidiously. Kat acknowledged the pleasure that Garson was giving Katherine—just a few months before, it would have been more than enough to fill the small space that sexuality took up in her busy life—but now it seemed . . . elementary: Elemental, even crudely reproductive. Without intelligence, drama, or elegance. It was as if she had been living in three dimensions while playing the games with her fierce lovers, and now she was fixed in just two dimensions. She was erotically flat lining.

It wasn't enough any longer. Garson could huff and puff, and eventually she would enjoy what in other times she would have considered a stellar orgasm. But she knew it wasn't even worth telling Buddy about such a mundane experience.

The evening sun was going down. She inhaled their sex smells, and the smell of grass, even the smells of the animals in the zoo. She patted Garson's bearded cheek politely, and waited for him to roll away from her. She didn't even want to talk with him.

She wanted the darkness.

37

Olivier decided to throw a party to celebrate the climb of *My Life as a Monster* to the top of the bestseller lists. He was pleased that he had managed to shift the focus of public interest in his book from Mammon to Eros. (An insect-friendly national news magazine had named him "The Most Disgusting Man In America," and he couldn't have been more flattered.) The party would be his farewell to America, and he wanted to depart with an appropriately erotic flourish. Then the monster would slip off on the Concorde.

Eulalie objected, of course. He planned to create one of his infamous Mazes for the party, and present it to the media people who'd assisted in the success of his book. She feared that his deliberate attempts to shock would be dangerous to him eventually. A puritan herself, she could smell a crowd of crusading, cross-burning, hypocritical puritans coming a mile away.

"They despise you for being rich and scandalous and rubbing it in their faces. Why do you insist on baiting them?"

"Because it's my nature, dear Eulalie. Call Katherine for me, so we can concoct an amusing guest list."

Olivier had come to admire Katherine's intelligence, and to rely on her advice. After she heard his ideas for the party, she suggested that he hold it at the Subterranean Club, thinking that at least there she could control whatever damage might ensue from presenting media people with the Maze. She was gold at GCI, but her new look irritated Christian; she didn't have his job yet. She would have to be careful, she knew. But another part of her—perhaps in response to the example of Olivier's boldness—simply said, I don't care what happens. There's no turning back for me. It was this part of her that told Olivier about her transformative experience with Star and Cyd. She suggested that there was a way he could make his party remembered for the lifetimes of his braver guests: Star could be present, tattooing blue butterflies as party favors.

Olivier roared his assent. The image of prominent television hosts potentially baring their buttocks for a tattoo was irresistible.

"Call him. Set it up."

She called back to tell him Star wouldn't do it. He was no sideshow attraction, no Coney Island assembly line mechanic.

"It's the artist syndrome, Olivier. You know about that."

"But what can we do?"

"You can go visit him. Anyway, I think you'll enjoy each other. You'll have a lot to talk about, I think."

Olivier drove the black Austin down to Houston Street that evening. When Eulalie made the appointment with Star for him, she reported that the man had demanded that he bring cash, so Olivier carried with him a briefcase containing enough one hundred dollar bills to convince a prince. He gave an urchin ten dollars to watch his car, pressed the button at ASTERION

STUDIOS, and walked up, prepared for an adventure.

He was greeted by the ugliest woman he'd seen since his arrival in New York. But when he looked into her slightly crossed eyes, he saw a vacancy that enflamed him. She was naked, except for a garter belt, stockings and high heels, but she was intimidating.

He walked into darkness, and an unnatural warmth. It felt as if bats were flying at his face, but when he put his arms up to ward them off, he struck at air. The woman took his arm and led him into candlelight. He sat on a leather couch and tried to blink away the blackness.

Then a large man appeared, a candle in one hand, a beer bottle in the other. Olivier could just make out his face, and the startling tattoo between his eyes. The man was angry, he sensed. But what did he care? He knew who he was.

"I am Olivier de Carlo," he told the man. "Katherine told me that you do tattoos. I am giving a party—at the Subterranean Club . . . Perhaps you've heard of me?"

The man belched, and nodded. The ugly red head crouched at his feet, like a dog that might be commanded to spring.

"You're the fucking frog who married Robin. I know all about you," he growled, and belched again. It was obvious that he was drunk, or crazy, but Olivier was not intimidated by him. He put the briefcase between them on a coffee table, and opened it.

"Katherine said you would require payment in advance for your services at my party." He was calm, he was smooth. Money had never failed him in any encounter.

Star contemplated the money. He bent his head to whisper in his assistant's ear, and she grinned. Olivier felt his insides tighten. Her grin was like a knife drawn across skin.

She knelt over the money on the coffee table, giving him a good view of her small naked breasts. He watched, stricken, as she plucked a hundred dollar bill from his treasure, held it over a candle, and used the flame to light the cigarette Star had placed in his mouth.

Such desecration! He was outraged. His heart raced.

"You cannot do this," he choked out, as the woman plucked another bill, and held it before the candle.

"Oh, I'm not doing this. This is my assistant, Cyd. Cyd, meet a rich man who thinks he knows something about sex."

What happened next shook Olivier's equilibrium. Star reached behind him and came up with an ugly-looking pistol that he pointed at Olivier. He blew a smoke ring.

"Fuck you and your party—here's one for Buddy Tate!"

He fired. Olivier ducked instinctively, and heard Star's drunken, raucous laughter. His ears rang with the pistol's report. He felt disoriented, as if he'd stepped into a parallel universe where money had no weight, and drunken madmen with pistols ruled. He'd wet himself.

"Now that I've got your attention, let's talk business," Star said calmly. Cyd had covered her ears, but she kept the unnerving smile on her face. "Don't worry, I won't shoot you. But if you get out of line, I'll sic Cyd on you. She'll bite your ball off, if I tell her to." Cyd was examining another bill.

It was no surprise for Olivier that Star knew about his monorchid condition. Everyone seemed to talk to everyone else who played the games. Everyone was "family"—a word he detested.

His sure gambler's instinct told him that Star made up his moves as the whim moved him. He would be a formidable opponent in any games they might play together, because of this unpredictability. It was a trait Olivier had often used to his own advantage.

But what did he want?

"You can burn the money if you like. There's plenty more," Olivier said disdainfully, guessing that only this attitude would gain him the advantage. He continued, apparently unruffled by the gun shot, his crotch warm with urine. "You are an artist who would add a great deal to my party. I'll pay you whatever you ask."

"I don't know. Bunch of creeps at a party, it's not my style."

"These will be some people you've heard of, I promise you." He described the party—elaborating on his concept of the Maze—and named the guests he would be inviting. "The exposure will make you famous."

"I'm already famous, with the kind of people I want to know," Star rumbled. "But it might be fun to prick those media pricks, you know?"

"You might start with me," Olivier said. Star's heavy eyebrows lifted in surprise. Olivier kept his gaze steady, certain that it was only by constantly challenging Star that he could gain the upper hand.

"Oh yeah? What did you have in mind?"

"A blue butterfly."

"Where'd you hear about that?"

"Oh, word gets around. I guess I'm the last to know."

"Where?"

"I want it where it flutters goodbye when I walk away."

Star snorted with amusement. By the time Olivier was stretched on the table with his wet pants off, they'd begun to form a friendship based on their similar natures. Cyd watched them.

"Buddy told me you were a heavy hitter."

"I respect your friend greatly."

"And you married crazy Robin? I guess I can see why. That spider woman must give you a run for your money."

"Alas, she will do very little for me."

"What do you mean? No nookie?" Star was incredulous.

"We have these . . . ordinary needs that she meets. But she will not put me to the test. It is frustrating."

He found the tattooing process stimulating, in a mild, non-specific way. He was more excited by his awareness that Cyd was watching them. He found himself strongly attracted to her. With his sensitivity to erotic possibilities, he recognized something in her that he needed. He was seldom wrong about these hunches.

Star asked what he meant by a "test." As he answered, his eyes went to Cyd, who crouched in the corner. She stared back.

"Certain people have gifts—erotic gifts. Most people who have these gifts—these talents, whatever you want to call it—are unaware of them. They succeed in repressing them, usually. Those who don't may become great courtesans, or street prostitutes, notable dominatrixes and gross perverts—as society calls them."

"Sounds like Buddy, all right. But what about Robin?"

"Oh, Miranda has the gift. But she refuses to use it with me—it's only happened once since I married her."

"That time with Buddy? When he said you were spying on them?"

"Yes. He brings it out in her. But the irony of my marital situation is that I want her to use her darkest passions on me—to test my limits—and she won't."

"Maybe she's afraid she'll flip out and—you know, what she did to her father, that evangelist prick. . . ."

"Just so. But I am not getting any younger. You see my body. I look at the future as years, not decades. I want this fulfillment before I die."

"Sounds like you'd rather die in a dungeon than in bed."

"You understand me, my artist friend. Exactly."

38

There is a lonely beach on the island of Tobago where groves of tall bamboo clack gently together when a sea breeze is blowing. Lizards sitting on flat rocks gaze out over the blue-green waves that roll in.

Miranda lay stretched out on a blanket on this beach, alone, bathing in the hot morning sun and reflecting on the course of events that had brought her to the island again.

Olivier's last surprise for her was his request for a divorce. He had taken her shopping, and had been unusually generous at Bergdorf's. After lunch, he told her that he had an urgent business meeting, and asked her to accompany him, since it wouldn't take long. The business meeting was with a prominent divorce lawyer, who pushed papers across his desk for her to sign.

She protested, of course, but Olivier demanded that she sign immediately. In return for her immediate co-operation, he offered her the house in Tobago, as well as a generous settlement. She could disappear into the Caribbean, where she would never be followed—either by her father's fanatical myrmidons, or the police. Robin Flood would be no more.

She signed. In the suite at the Gibbons-Wakely, she packed her bags. Eulalie smirked victoriously.

Just like that, she was free. No more Olivier, no more Buddy. If Kat wanted to come down for a visit, they would play lightly and discreetly, keeping things under control. Remembering what they'd done with Buddy, she felt as if fate had pulled her back from the precipice.

She would be able to amuse herself in Tobago. The islanders were uninhibited and energetic in bed, and there was a constant influx of European tourists from whom she could pick and choose her dalliances.

There was Redmon, of course—who at this moment was running down the beach toward her, late for their reunion. She stood up to remove her bikini top, to give him a proper greeting. She would forgive him this time, but he would need to be disciplined if they were to continue together.

39

When Kat led Buddy down into the Subterranean Club on the evening of Olivier's party, she was wearing the tight, shiny black rubber suit and boots she'd worn on her first visit, but she was no longer playing a role. She was queen of the night.

She had decided to put Buddy on a leash because she knew his attraction to trouble. Besides his studded dog collar, he wore black leather gloves and chaps so he could walk on all fours on the sticky floor. His muscular rump bore the branding of the blue butterfly. His penis was confined in a tribally carved, Amazonian penis sheath, which was tied with leather laces up against his abdomen.

He was a good dog, obedient and attentive to his mistress, who had painstakingly taught him the meditation of submission to her will. Nevertheless, she had placed a muzzle on him, because then he looked like he might bite. *He won't*, she thought, *but I might*. The club was crowded with players and posers, but the dominatrix with the large dog was given respectful space.

The regulars were there, and there were special guests

who had traveled from Europe for Olivier's party—and another chance to crawl the Maze.

Limousines were delivering the invited representatives of American megamedia who had contributed to making *My Life as a Monster* such a scandalous success. Armed with their reflexively cynical puritanism, they had come to see for themselves Olivier de Carlo make a fool of himself in a shady sex club. Pundits and talk show hosts, publishers and reviewers, publicity people and money people, they were drawn inexorably by the irresistible combination of money and sex to the spectacle of the season.

They were greeted by the elegantly tailored Olivier de Carlo, who introduced them to his fiancée, Cyd. Defiantly slutty in her bustier, hot pants and collar, Cyd was at ease in her role as hostess. Olivier was amused to see her stare down women in designer outfits. Her capacities were a constant surprise to him.

But then she had fascinated him from the first. She'd more than lived up to his expectations since the night at Star's when she left with him. (When Star complained that she was deserting him, she had replied with laconic *sang froid*, "every deal changes.") A truly amazing woman, full of surprise and caprice—and, far from being ugly, as he first thought, she now seemed to him exotically beautiful.

She escorted their media guests through the crowd of players to the Maze, which had been set up on a floor below the club. She left them at the door to the Maze, and returned to Olivier's side.

From Buddy's eye level, they were all assholes, so he kept his attention on his mistress. She was imperious, unreachable, beautiful—and she had a use for him. She was his, so long as he submitted.

Olivier, too, thought Kat looked regal.

"You have been of enormous help to me," he told her. "Everyone is reading my book. Some are even reading it for the right reasons. Why don't you come to Europe with Cyd and me?"

"And Eulalie?" Kat shook her head.

"The poor dear is always with me, yes," he shrugged. *"Ma mere."*

"No. I like it here. I like what's happening now. I even like my job."

"Perhaps I might help you with that? Allow me to do something."

"Well. . . ." She smiled wickedly. He understood.

"Of course," he nodded—having met Christian in the GCI offices. "Consider it done."

The party had heated up. His invited guests were either gawking at various scenes, standing at the bar feeling awkward, or lost in the Maze. Cyd went to see what was happening there, and returned to report to Olivier, "They're screaming down there. They're running. You'd better get ready."

Olivier smiled thinly. It was the smile of a man who had just cornered the market on outrage.

"Surely, you're exaggerating," he purred.

But she wasn't. From his position at his mistress's side, Buddy had a good view of the lower halves of a lot of indignant people shouting at Olivier. Their knee movements were jerky, and their hip movements were stiff.

Star appeared out of the smoke, his broad tattooed chest glistening with sweat. He chatted with Kat about the party, and about some of the guests he'd tattooed, but he was eyeing Buddy, who sat on his haunches, at heel. He shook his head.

"You follow your dick, look where it leads you," he said.

Restrained from answering by the muzzle, Buddy simply waggled his hips in reply, looking up at his friend with steady, patient, unknowable eyes.

40

On the prowl, Kat stood at the bar of the Subterranean Club, scanning the darkened main room for signs of life. It was late, and she should have been tired, but it was Easter, and she felt new. She was optimistic enough to hope that she might find a player worthy of her energy and imagination.

The media-ocracy had fled the apostate temple of players, and Olivier had whisked Cyd off in a limousine to never-never land—to a place over the rainbow of pain from which they might never emerge. She had asked Star to take Buddy home, and kennel him in the cage. Buddy's muzzle had been a wise precaution, as he sorely protested their separation.

She was alone, but she did not feel desperate. How could she? Each thing arrived in its time; what was needed, appeared. So she studied each man and woman still engaged in the endless scenes in the smoky club. Now the regular performers were taking the stage here and there, like candles in the darkness. She was fascinated, as always—as she had been from the first—by the constantly shifting tableaux of need and desire. She saw how the subtleties of passion and technique made sense in the context of the darkness. How roles changed with the needs of the script.

Buddy had shown her how much real players were willing to risk. He'd taught her that most people didn't know what they wanted, and were too frightened to find out. They dabbled in the dark games and then drew back, fearful of being pulled in.

She ordered another vodka, drinking an icy double down without taking her eyes from the room. She noticed a flurry of movement at the door, and peered through the haze of smoke at this late arrival.

His smile ate up the room, ate up the darkness, sucked up her tiredness and dissipated it. He was a large black man in a leather gladiator's outfit. His skin of ebony and dark honey glistened. His features shone with the confidence of a young boxer who's just won a championship fight.

He saw Kat and began to move toward her through the crowd of players. He'd shown up, once again, she knew.

Not *him*, but one like him.

Available now

The Captive
by Anonymous

When a wealthy Enlish man-about-town attempts to make advances to the beautiful twenty-year-old debutante Caroline Martin, she haughtily repels him. As revenge, he pays a white-slavery ring £30,000 to have Caroline abducted and spirited away to the remote Atlas Mountains of Morocco. There the mistress of the ring and her sinister assistant Jason begin Caroline's education—an abduction designed to break her will and prepare her for her mentor.

———————

Available now

Captive II
by Richard Manton

Following the best-selling novel, *The Captive*, this sequel is set among the subtropical provinces of Cheluna, where white slavery remains an institution to this day. Brigid, with her dancing girl figure and sweeping tresses of red hair, has caused the prosecution of a rich admirer. As retribution, he employs the underground organization Rio 9 to abduct and transport her to Cambina Alta Plantation. Naked and bound before the Sadism of Col. Manrique and the perversities of the Comte de Zantra, Brigid endures an education in submission. Her training continues until she is ready to be the slave of the man who has chosen her.

———————

Available now

Captive III: The Perfumed Trap
by Anonymous

The story of slavery and passionate training described first-hand in the spirited correspondence of two wealthy cousins, Alec and Miriam. The power wielded by them over the girls who cross their paths leads them beyond Cheluna to the remote settlement of Cambina Alta and a life of plantation discipline. On the way, Alec's passion for Julie, a golden-haired nymph, is rivaled by Miriam's disciplinary zeal for Jenny, a rebellious young woman under correction at a police barracks.

Forthcoming

Captive IV: The Eyes Behind the Mask
by Anonymous

The Captives of Cheluna feel a dread fascination for the boy whose duty it is to chastise. This narrative follows a masked apprentice who obeys his master's orders without pity or restraint. Emma Smith's birching would cause a reform school scandal. Secret additions to the frenzy of nineteen-year-old Karen and Noreen mingle the boy's fierce passion with lascivious punishment. Mature young women like Jenny Woodward pay dearly for defying their master, whose masked servant also prints the marks of slavery on Lesley Hollingsworth, following *Captive II*. The untrained and the self-assured alike learn to shiver, as they lie waiting, under the caress of the eyes behind the mask.

———

Available now

Captive V: The Soundproof Dream
by Richard Manton

Beauty lies in bondage everywhere in the tropical island of Cheluna. Joanne, a 19-year old rebel, is sent to detention on Krater Island where obedience and discipline occupy the secret hours of night. Like the dark beauty Shirley Wood and blond shopgirl Maggie Turnbull, Jo is subjected to unending punishment. When her Krater Island training is complete, Jo's fate is Metron, the palace home of the strange Colonel Mantrique.

Available now

Images of Ironwood
by Don Winslow

Ironwood. The very name of that unique institution remains strongly evocative, even to this day. In this, the third volume of the famous Ironwood trilogy, the reader is once again invited to share in the Ironwood experience. *Images of Ironwood* presents selected scenes of unrelenting sensuality, of erotic longing, and occasionally, of those bizarre proclivities which touch the outer fringe of human sexuality.

In these pages we renew our acquaintance with James, the lusty entrepreneur who now directs the Ironwood enterprise; with his bevy of young female students being trained in the many ways of love; and with Cora Blasingdale, the cold remote mistress of discipline. The images presented here capture the essence of the Ironwood experience.

———

Available Now

Ironwood
by Don Winslow

The harsh reality of disinheritance and poverty vanish from the world of our young narrator, James, when he discovers he's in line for a choice position at an exclusive and very strict school for girls. Ironwood becomes for him a fantastic dream world where discipline knows few boundaries, and where his role as master affords him free reign with the willing, well-trained and submissive young beauties in his charge. As overseer of Ironwood, Cora Blasingdale is well-equipped to keep her charges in line. Under her guidance the saucy girls are put through their paces and tamed. And for James, it seems, life has just begun.

☙ TITLES IN THE SHADOW LANE SERIES ☙
FROM BLUE MOON BOOKS

Available now

SHADOW LANE

In a small New England village, four spirited young women explore the romance of discipline with their lovers. Laura's husband is handsome but terribly strict, leaving her no choice but to rebel. Damaris is a very bad girl until detective Flagg takes her in hand. Susan simultaneously begins her freshman year at college and her odyssey in the scene with two charming older men. Marguerite can't decide whether to remain dreamily submissive or become a goddess.

———

Available now

SHADOW LANE II
Return to Random Point

All Susan Ross ever wanted was a handsome and masterful lover who would turn her over his knee now and then without trying to control her life. She ends up with three of them in this second installment of the ongoing chronicle of romantic discipline, set in a village on Cape Cod.

———

Available now

SHADOW LANE III
The Romance of Discipline

Mischievous Susan Ross, now at Vassar, continues to exasperate Anthony Newton, while pursuing other dominant men. Heroically proportioned Michael Flagg proves capable but bossy, while handsome Marcus Gower has one too many demands. Dominating her girlfriend Diana brings Susan unexpected satisfaction, but playing top is work and so she turns her submissive over to the boys. Susan then inspires her adoring servant Dennis to revolt against his own submissive nature and turn his young mistress over his knee.

Order These Selected Blue Moon Titles

Souvenirs From a Boarding School $7.95	Shades of Singapore $7.95
The Captive $7.95	Images of Ironwood $7.95
Ironwood Revisited $7.95	What Love $7.95
Sundancer $7.95	Sabine $7.95
Julia $7.95	An English Education $7.95
The Captive II $7.95	The Encounter $7.95
Shadow Lane $7.95	Tutor's Bride $7.95
Belle Sauvage $7.95	A Brief Education $7.95
Shadow Lane III $7.95	Love Lessons $7.95
My Secret Life $9.95	Shogun's Agent $7.95
Our Scene $7.95	The Sign of the Scorpion $7.95
Chrysanthemum, Rose & the Samurai $7.95	Women of Gion $7.95
Captive V $7.95	Mariska I $7.95
Bombay Bound $7.95	Secret Talents $7.95
Sadopaideia $7.95	Beatrice $7.95
The New Story of O $7.95	S&M: The Last Taboo $8.95
Shadow Lane IV $7.95	"Frank" & I $7.95
Beauty in the Birch $7.95	Lament $7.95
Laura $7.95	The Boudoir $7.95
The Reckoning $7.95	The Bitch Witch $7.95
Ironwood Continued $7.95	Story of O $5.95
In a Mist $7.95	Romance of Lust $9.95
The Prussian Girls $7.95	Ironwood $7.95
Blue Velvet $7.95	Virtue's Rewards $5.95
Shadow Lane V $7.95	The Correct Sadist $7.95
Deep South $7.95	The New Olympia Reader $15.95

Visit our website at www.bluemoonbooks.com

ORDER FORM
Attach a separate sheet for additional titles.

Title	Quantity	Price
_____	____	_____
_____	____	_____
_____	____	_____
_____	____	_____

Shipping and Handling (see charges below) _____

Sales tax (in CA and NY) _____

Total _____

Name _____

Address _____

City _____ State _____ Zip _____

Daytime telephone number _____

❑ Check ❑ Money Order (US dollars only. No COD orders accepted.)

Credit Card # _____ Exp. Date _____

❑ MC ❑ VISA ❑ AMEX

Signature _____

(if paying with a credit card you must sign this form.)

Shipping and Handling charges:*

Domestic: $4 for 1st book, $.75 each additional book. International: $5 for 1st book, $1 each additional book
*rates in effect at time of publication. Subject to Change.

Mail order to Publishers Group West, Attention: Order Dept., 1700 Fourth St., Berkeley, CA 94710, or fax to (510) 528-3444.

PLEASE ALLOW 4-6 WEEKS FOR DELIVERY. ALL ORDERS SHIP VIA 4TH CLASS MAIL.

Look for Blue Moon Books at your favorite local bookseller or from your favorite online bookseller.